"Rachel…"

It was a very different sound. One that seemed shaken and vulnerable. Impossible! Gabriel vulnerable? Never!

With a small choking cry she caught her arms up around his neck and pulled his face down to hers. Instantly it was as if she was bathed in lightning from her head to her toes.

There was nothing vulnerable about the way Gabriel's lips took hers. His kisses were greedy, seeking, *demanding* a response she gave willingly. Her mouth opened under his, yielding to the intimate caress she craved every bit as much as he did.

A moment later he wrenched his head up, pulling away from her with a ferocity that tore agonizingly at every nerve.

"Gabriel…?"

"No! This has to stop right now."

"Stop? Why? Why must it stop?"

KATE WALKER was born in Nottinghamshire, England, but as she grew up in Yorkshire she has always felt that her roots were there. She met her husband at university and originally worked as a children's librarian, but after the birth of her son she returned to her old childhood love of writing. When she's not working she divides her time between her family, their four cats and her interests of embroidery, antiques, film and theater, and, of course, reading.

Books by Kate Walker

HARLEQUIN PRESENTS®

1921—THE UNEXPECTED CHILD
2035—THE GROOM'S REVENGE

Kate Walker

THE TEMPTATION GAME

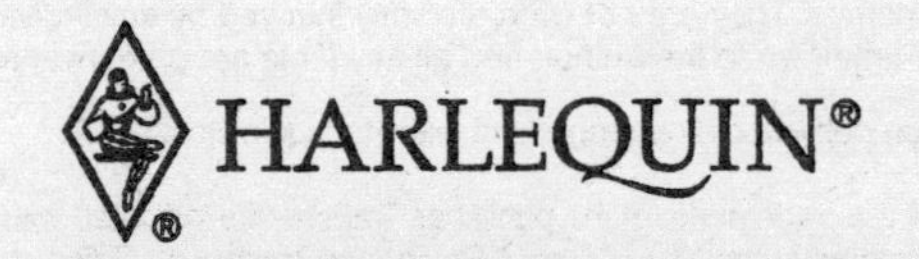

TORONTO • NEW YORK • LONDON
AMSTERDAM • PARIS • SYDNEY • HAMBURG
STOCKHOLM • ATHENS • TOKYO • MILAN • MADRID
PRAGUE • WARSAW • BUDAPEST • AUCKLAND

For Steve
With all my love
for this special anniversary

ISBN 0-373-18728-9

THE TEMPTATION GAME

First North American Publication 2000.

This edition published by arrangement with Harlequin Books S.A.

Visit us at www.romance.net

Printed in U.S.A.

CHAPTER ONE

'HE'S here!'

Rachel dropped the corner of the curtain she had been holding away from the window and stepped back hastily, her jerky movement a clear indicator of her unsettled frame of mind. With a nervous hand she swept her chestnut hair back from her face, anxiety turning her eyes to the colour of rain-washed slate instead of their usual pale, silvery grey.

'Right on time, of course.'

But then, Gabriel had always been scrupulously punctual, she acknowledged inwardly. He had only ever been late once to her knowledge, and that occasion had been planned with a cold ruthlessness that still made her shiver to remember it.

Whatever else she could accuse him of—and there was plenty that came easily to mind—keeping her waiting was not one of his faults.

'Come away from that window, Rachel!'

Her mother's concern was voiced in an urgent whisper, almost as if she feared she could actually be heard by the man who was now emerging from the sleek dark blue Jaguar parked by the front door.

'If he should see you looking...'

'This window wouldn't be visible from inside his car,' Rachel reassured her, but she moved all the same.

He might not have been able to see her before, she told herself, struggling to control the painful, uneven thudding of her heart, but now that he was actually on the doorstep it was a very different matter.

A strong sense of self-preservation warred uncomfortably with an almost overwhelming curiosity, something she wasn't really prepared to admit to, even to herself, and it took all her strength to squash it down firmly. She didn't want it to look as if she cared about his arrival, as if it mattered to her at all. She would see soon enough just what had become of him in the four and a half years he had been away.

The sound of the doorbell ringing through the house made the two women tense, and in the silence that followed it they heard the housekeeper's footsteps crossing the tiled hall.

'Oh, Rachel, I don't know how I'm going to cope with this, I really don't!' Lydia Tiernan's voice slid up and down like a radio on which the volume control had broken. 'I always vowed that if that man ever set foot in this house again I would leave immediately. I would rather *die* than live under the same roof as him!'

'I expect that would be exactly what he'd want, Mum.' Rachel's tone was bitter. 'Oh, not the dying bit—though I'm sure he would see that as the answer to all his problems. But even to talk about leaving would just be playing right into his hands.'

'Running away, you mean?'

'And leaving him in possession. And, possession being nine-tenths of the law…'

She could see that she didn't have to go any further. Her mother's expression had changed perceptibly, her mouth firming and a new light of determination burning in the eyes that were a couple of shades darker than her daughter's.

'Well, I don't intend letting grasping Gabriel get away with *anything*, let alone nine-tenths of what is rightfully mine,' she declared, with more determination than Rachel had seen her display for days. 'He has more than enough of his own, and I won't—'

She broke off sharply as a knock at the door prefaced the housekeeper's entrance.

'Excuse me, ma'am,' Mrs Reynolds announced, 'you have a visitor—Mr Gabriel Tiernan.'

The name was spoken with such a note of drama that it had the effect of a full-scale fanfare heralding at the very least the arrival of a major member of the royal family. So much so that Rachel was gripped by an irrational urge to bob a curtsy in the direction of the tall, dark man who now appeared in the doorway.

But just one look at his face drove any such thought from her head. Because the problem was that four and a half years had hardly changed Gabriel Tiernan at all. He still had the same instant impact when he walked into a room. He still dominated his surroundings in a way that made his tall, rangy form seem bigger, more forceful than it actually was.

His eyes were the deepest, darkest brown that was possible without actually being black, his hair almost an exact match. His face had always reminded her of a Dürer engraving—all strong lines and planes, no hint of softness except in the mouth that was both cruel and sensual at the same time.

The intervening years hadn't added a single ounce to his spare frame. If anything, he was leaner and tougher looking than ever. He was all male, hard and unyielding through and through, as she knew to her cost.

Simply seeing him, Rachel found herself prey to a rush of burning hatred dangerously blended with a bitter pain that was so potent it actually rocked her back on her heels. It took all her strength not to cry out, an even more ruthless control to resist the urge to turn on her heel, stalk out of the room and refuse to acknowledge him with so much as a word.

Instead, she forced herself to meet his dark brown gaze head-on, keeping her own eyes carefully blank. Tossing back the soft burnished waves of her hair and lifting her chin defiantly, she swallowed down the angry, accusatory words she was tempted to fling at that proudly held dark head.

'Mr Tiernan.'

The idea had been to inject her expression with as

much hauteur as she could drag up. She wanted to freeze him to the spot, watch him splinter into shards like a shattered icicle.

Unfortunately the effect was not at all what she had hoped for. Gabriel Tiernan looked remarkably unfrozen as he shrugged himself out of his rain-spattered trench-coat before handing it to the housekeeper with a nod of dismissal. Instead, he switched on the sort of wide, brilliant smile that would have melted any degree of frost.

'Hello, kid,' he drawled, the evidence of his time in America accenting his deep voice. 'It's good to see you again.'

'I'm afraid the feeling isn't mutual.'

The words slipped out before she had a chance to consider whether they were wise or not. She was beginning to feel slightly punch-drunk, trying to adjust to the dazzling effect of that smile, the appalling, head-swimming reaction it had sparked off deep inside her.

'And I do wish you wouldn't call me kid!'

'Why is that, I wonder? Could it be because you're so obviously not a child any more?'

It was meant to provoke and it succeeded only too well. All the more so when it was accompanied by such a blatantly assessing scrutiny of her from the top of her head to the soles of her shoes and back again. The sweep of his gaze seared over the simple navy shift dress, seeming to scorch her skin where it touched. She had to force herself to bite back the furious retort she longed to fling straight into his arrogantly handsome face.

This was no time to declare that she could never be pleased to see him. That although they might have shared a home for almost three years they had never been anything remotely like a family. If she had ever been anything more then he would never have treated her as appallingly as he had done, never have abused her trust and destroyed her innocence.

'If you mean that I'm no longer nineteen, then you're right. I've grown up a lot while you've been away. And, by the way,' she added stiffly, 'my name is Rachel. I would prefer you to use it.'

A brief nod of his dark head was his only response. He seemed to have tired of needling her. Or perhaps he had simply recalled the reason why he was here at all.

Whatever his thinking, the taunting gleam died from his ebony eyes as he turned away from her, glancing towards where her mother sat stiffly upright on the blue silk-covered settee.

'Lydia.'

It was a brusquely formal acknowledgement of the older woman's presence—another, even briefer inclination of his head his only greeting. He made no move to come forward or hold out his hand to her, obviously knowing that it would never be taken. Her mother would simply ignore any such pretence of courtesy.

'May I offer you my most sincere condolences on your loss.'

At his words, Rachel's heart beat painfully in her chest, depriving her of a couple of breaths so that she had to gasp sharply in reaction.

Gabriel Tiernan offering her mother sympathy! If she hadn't been so very wide awake she might have suspected she was dreaming.

But then, of course, bereavement did strange things to people. A sudden twist of the nerves in her stomach added to her jittery, uncertain mood, making her wonder just where that thought might lead. Was it possible that after all this time old wounds could finally be healed, bridges be rebuilt? Could it be that the dreams she had had when she was younger of her complicated, fractured family finally making peace with each other might actually come true?

But that hope lasted only as long as it took her mother to respond.

'Thank you.'

As an acknowledgement it was as stiff as Gabriel's own, and Lydia's grey eyes didn't even glance in his direction. Instead, they were firmly and discouragingly fixed on a point on the blue and cream carpet some inches from her own feet.

The dream of peace faded as swiftly as it had come. The battle-lines were still clearly drawn, defences firmly in place.

But someone had to do what was right. After all, no matter what she thought of this man, when her mother had lost her second husband, he had lost his father.

'And our sympathies to you too, Gabriel,' she said hastily, concerned to find that her voice sounded rusty and uneven, as if it hadn't been used for some time.

There was no softening of his expression, no perceptible warmth in the black-coffee-coloured gaze he turned on her. If anything, it seemed as if his features had hardened until it appeared that they had been weathered out of granite by the winter wind and rain.

'How very gracious of you.'

There was a dangerous undertone to the silky words, one that sent shivers of reaction down Rachel's spine. It reminded her of just why she had dreaded this day for so long, why she had feared the events that must, inevitably, bring him back into her life once more.

'So, now that we've got the polite conventions out of the way, perhaps we could talk practicalities? Exactly what arrangements have you made for my father's funeral?'

My father. He didn't need to say anything more. Those two words made it only too plain how separate he believed them to be from him. They were simply hangers-on, no real part of his life.

So much for her youthful dreams. She had only been deluding herself to think they might ever come true, and now she knew that they were no longer what she really wanted anyway. She was no longer the same person who had had those naive hopes. Gabriel himself had forced her to change sides.

In the private civil war that was laughingly termed her

family life, she had gone from being wholeheartedly and enthusiastically *for* him to being totally and immovably *against*.

He was going to hate them even more when he discovered the full truth.

That thought made her feel as if an electrical shock had just burned through her, so that she knew she had to get out of the room or she would scream, or shout—react in some wholly inappropriate manner. She had known that Gabriel's arrival would be a strain, but she had never anticipated that it would be quite this bad.

'You've had a long journey,' she put in hastily. 'You must be tired. Can I get you anything?'

'Coffee would be nice.'

Only the faintest flicker of a glance in her direction acknowledged her intervention. His attention was concentrated on her mother, who had finally turned to look at him and was regarding him with the sort of fascinated wariness that is normally reserved for a venomous snake, poised about to strike.

'Anything to eat?' Rachel was already heading for the door.

'Nothing—thanks,' he added belatedly, apparently only just realising that he wasn't speaking to one of his employees in the American offices of Tiernan's Jewellery. 'Just coffee.'

Escaping from the sitting room was like going from the overheated atmosphere of a sauna into the clear, fresh cool of a rain-washed garden. Only with the door closed firmly behind her did Rachel realise just how difficult she had been finding it to breathe in the strained, tight atmosphere she had left behind.

It took several deep, calming gulps of air from a nearby open window before she felt calm enough to move again, turning and heading for the kitchen.

It would have been simpler to pass on the request for coffee to the family housekeeper, so sparing herself the small duty. But preparing the drink herself gave her the perfect excuse to stay away for long enough to take a much needed breather. Time to calm her thudding pulse, restore some order to her jangled thoughts.

Just what had happened to the past four and a half years? she couldn't help wondering, her hands busy with the simple tasks of spooning coffee into the filter machine, filling the water tank. It was as if, in the moment that Gabriel had walked into the room, the intervening four and a half years had evaporated. She was once more the unsophisticated nineteen-year-old he had last seen, a prey to the emotional roller-coaster of adolescence and naively believing herself in love for the first time.

Love. The word rang inside her head, as hollow-toned as a death knell. Which, of course, was just how it had been, marking the death of her ideals, her innocence. Gabriel had taken her dreams in his powerful, heartless grip and crushed the life out of them for ever.

'No! I won't even *think* of it!'

Spinning away from the worktop, she looked for something to distract herself from the pain of memories she had hoped were long since buried. Opening cupboards at random, she found a selection of packets of biscuits, pulled one out, ripping off the wrapping, and emptied the contents onto a plate.

He had said that he didn't want to eat, but the tray would look better with more than just coffee on it.

Gabriel must have the hearing of a hunting cat, she realised when she took the tray back across the hall. She hadn't even reached the sitting-room door before it was pulled open and her burden taken from her.

'I'll carry that.'

'There's no need…'

Her protest died when she realised his words had been a declaration, not a suggestion, and there was nothing she could do but concede as graciously as possible. She watched in silence as he placed the tray on a coffee table in the centre of the room.

'Nothing for either of you?' His gesture took in the single cup and saucer.

'We've only just had lunch. What is it?' she questioned in response to his sudden change of expression, to the unexpected smile that curled the corners of the mouth that up until now had been tightly compressed to hold back any revelation of his feelings.

'My favourites.' He held up a biscuit and crunched a small piece appreciatively. 'You remembered.'

Rachel realised what she had just done. When Gabriel had lived at home, he had always had a weakness for these particular oat and honey cookies. Made by a small local bakery, they came very close to tasting home made, and in the past he had only had to express a fancy for some to have her volunteering to go to the shop for him.

Silently she cursed her subconscious for leading her to select that particular packet from the assortment in the cupboard. She knew only too well just what interpretation Gabriel was capable of putting onto the simple action.

'On the contrary,' she declared stiffly. 'They were the only biscuits we had in. I forgot to ask Mrs Reynolds to put some on the shopping list, so it was Hobson's choice.'

Refusing to meet his eyes, afraid of the sardonically sceptical look she suspected must be lurking in their ebony depths, she deliberately turned her attention to her mother instead.

'Are you all right, Mum?' She moved to sit beside Lydia on the settee, taking her hand. 'Can I get you anything?'

'Nothing, thank you.'

It came out in a ragged sigh. Lydia's grey eyes were red-rimmed and moist, and as she spoke she pressed a fine cotton handkerchief to the corner of one of them, wiping away one of the tears that were always so close to the surface.

'I couldn't touch a thing.'

'Perhaps a lie-down would be a good idea. Even if you don't sleep, the rest would do you good.'

Rachel was painfully aware of just how little sleep her mother had had since that appalling morning when the police had arrived on the doorstep with the news of a multiple pile-up on the motorway.

'That is, if you've talked over everything you need to discuss?'

The last remark was directed at Gabriel, who had filled his coffee cup and was now standing silently—a dark, watchful observer of the scene before him.

'We've covered all the important points,' he returned coolly. 'Anything else can wait until later.'

'Then if you'll excuse us...?'

His nod of agreement, like his words a moment earlier, had the blend of condescension and graciousness that one might expect from a lord of the manor giving a lowly serf permission to act with his approval.

Typical Gabriel, Rachel reflected cynically. He had always regarded herself and her mother as intruders, and had treated them as such. For a short time she had been accepted, even offered a degree of affection, but Lydia had always been shown the sort of arrogant indifference that it now seemed they were both to be subjected to.

'I won't be a moment.' She was helping her mother to her feet as she spoke. 'Help yourself to more coffee if you'd like.'

It was pitched deliberately to match his own cool tone, and she knew that the pointed provocation wasn't lost on him as a dangerous flame of response flared in his eyes. He didn't like it. Not one bit.

The feeling that that thought brought grew more pronounced when she acknowledged that he was going to like it even less when he discovered the full truth about what had happened in the past two days. She was going to have to tell him that truth very soon. The longer she delayed, the worse it would inevitably be.

It took only a few minutes to settle her mother in the

first-floor bedroom, drawing the curtains to block out the spring sunshine that poured in through the large bay window.

'Try and rest, Mum,' she advised softly. 'I'll bring a tray of tea up in a couple of hours or so.'

Already the older woman's eyes were closing. The events of the past couple of days had drained all her strength and she was exhausted. But there was obviously something still fretting at her.

'Gabriel...'

'Don't worry,' Rachel reassured her. 'I'll handle Gabriel.'

The words seemed to trail after her as she descended the stairs, spinning round her head in a mocking echo that questioned the false confidence of her assertion.

When had she ever 'handled' Gabriel? When had anyone? He was a law unto himself and always had been. Even his father had never been able to keep him on any sort of a tight rein. Like a wayward stallion, he had always fought to be given his head.

Pausing at the door to the sitting room, she drew a deep breath and squared her shoulders purposefully. This would take careful handling.

She knew only too well what interpretation Gabriel would put on things, the scheming and machination he would believe was behind all that had happened. She would need to take it slowly, choose her words carefully.

But every reasoned phrase, every carefully thought out explanation, was driven from her thoughts the moment that she opened the door.

With his shoes kicked off and left just where they had fallen, Gabriel had flung himself down onto the elegant settee. His long legs were stretched out in front of him, resting on the elegant brocade cushions, and his tie had been tugged loose at his throat. He had also unfastened the top two buttons of his shirt, and another cushion supported his dark head.

His sprawled posture looked comfortable and relaxed,

and with his eyes closed he might almost have been asleep. But in one hand was a large tumbler containing a generous amount of what was obviously his father's favourite whisky, taken from the drinks cabinet on the opposite side of the room.

Anger and resentment boiled up inside Rachel like lava inside a volcano. It spilled out into her thoughts and actions in seconds, pushing her to march furiously into the room, letting the door slam to behind her.

'Make yourself at home, why don't you?' she snapped. 'Is there anything else you'd like?'

Heavy lids lifted lazily, and she was subjected to a slow, indolent survey that did nothing to ease her ruffled feelings.

'I'm fine, thanks,' he drawled smoothly. 'Or I will be once I've downed this.'

One long-fingered hand raised the elegant crystal in a parody of a goodwill toast.

'Care to join me?'

Care to join…! He was acting as if it was his house. He thought it *was* his house—that was the problem.

'In the middle of the afternoon? No, thanks! I've no wish to get roaring drunk!'

A deeply unfortunate comment, that, bringing instantly to mind the occasion four and a half years before when, decidedly tiddly on champagne, she had made perhaps the worst mistake of her life.

It was too late now to realise that it had been another agonisingly sharp reminder of that occasion, the only time she had ever seen him asleep before, that had pushed her into losing her temper. Foolishly, she had let it ruin her resolve to take things carefully.

'My, you have got your knickers in a twist!'

Lazily Gabriel levered himself upright and took another sip of his drink.

'It's only one whisky, for God's sake! And after the journey I've just had, I reckon I deserve one.'

'Oh, I'm sure it was hellish!' Overwrought emotions

drove her to forget her concerns of a moment before. 'Luxury class all the way, and the Atlantic's only a hop, skip and a jump on Concorde! You have no idea at all how real people travel!'

The dark look he shot her over the rim of his glass threatened to drain all the fire from her anger. She was only too aware of the fact it was really nothing more than a protective armour around feelings that were too much in turmoil to let him see. A sharp twist of unease tightened all the nerves in her stomach, drying her throat painfully.

'Not pleased to see me, then, I take it?' he murmured in an injured tone. But it was obvious that the hurt that was communicated by his voice, his wounded expression, was deliberately assumed, an act carefully put on for her benefit.

His mockery seemed to scour off a protective layer of skin, leaving her more vulnerable than ever to the pain of memories she had tried to hide from herself. Gabriel's reappearance in her life had stirred them up again, pushing them to the surface of her mind once more.

'Not pleased at all!' She flung the words at his darkly watchful face. 'If you want the truth, I would much rather you had stayed away for good. You must know you're not wanted here, that—'

'He *was* my father,' Gabriel inserted quietly into her tirade, stopping it mid-flow.

This time his pain was only too genuine. It was there in the rawness of his eyes, the way his skin was drawn tight over his strongly carved cheekbones. Seeing it, Rachel felt the prick of her conscience.

'Oh, Gabriel! I'm so sorry!'

Acting on pure instinct, she moved swiftly to sit beside him on the settee, her hand going out in a silent gesture of sympathy to curl over his where it lay on his knee.

'I should have thought. I know just what you're going through.'

For a long-drawn-out moment Gabriel let her hand lie there, staring down at it with dark, unreadable eyes. Then suddenly he gave an abrupt, violent movement and jerked himself free, pushing her sympathy away with a brutal carelessness.

'Do you really?' he demanded with a savage violence that terrified her. 'Do you really know *anything* of what I feel?'

'Of course I do!' The cruelty of his rejection mixed with her own private thoughts to produce a volatile cocktail of emotions. 'Greg meant a lot to me too. He was the only father I ever knew!'

But already Gabriel had got to his feet, tossing the remainder of his drink down his throat with total carelessness as to its effect. And suddenly Rachel knew that if she didn't tell him now, she never would. The thought of the possible consequences if he learned the facts from anyone else drove all thought of dodging the issue from her mind.

'Gabriel, there's something you must know,' she managed, addressing his broad, stiffly uncommunicative back.

If he turned, she wouldn't be able to continue. She knew she would never dare to say this to his face, aware of just how much he would hate it.

'It's about Greg—your father—and my mother. They—they were married on Friday night.'

She got the words out just in time. As the last one died away he whirled round to face her again. In his expression was everything she'd most dreaded she would see.

CHAPTER TWO

'THEY—'

The glass was slammed down onto the marble mantelpiece with a jarring crash.

'They were *what*?'

For all that he hadn't raised his voice above a dangerous whisper, Gabriel's words still had the force of violent blows, making Rachel shrink back against the cushions, fearful of the terrible emotion she could see in his eyes.

She had never seen him like this in her life before. Not even seven years before, when he and his father had clashed so appallingly following Gregory Tiernan's announcement that he was moving Lydia and her sixteen-year-old daughter into his London home. She had been terrified of him then, but it was nothing when compared to this.

And the only other times he had let slip the urbane mask he usually wore had been in two very different situations. One she couldn't bear even to bring to mind, and the other couldn't have been further from this. Then he had been coldly, cruelly indifferent, a man of ice, not the raging figure of fury now standing before her.

'Gabriel...' She tried, but her voice failed her before the dark blaze of his eyes.

'They were married, you said!'

Powerful hands closed over her arms, yanking her out of her seat until she was hard up against him. She was so close that she could feel the warmth of his skin, see his chest rise and fall with the ragged tenor of his breathing, sense the almost brutal control with which he held himself barely in check.

'*Married.* Is this true?'

'Yes...'

It was all Rachel could manage. The fire in those deep eyes seemed to have dried her throat, so that her voice croaked embarrassingly.

Those hard-fingered hands dug into her flesh, their cruel grip bruisingly painful on her arms, but she found herself praying that he would not let her go. If he did then she was convinced that her unsteady legs would not support her and she would collapse in a pathetic and humiliating heap at his feet.

'This is the absolute truth?'

'Of course it is!' At last, provoked by his obvious disbelief, she found herself able to respond more forcefully. 'What do you think I am? A liar?'

She even managed to drag up from somewhere the strength to wrench herself away from him, twisting out of his arms with an effort that took her halfway across the room.

'Have I ever lied to you before? And do you think that I'd start with something as important as this? Do you really believe this is something I'd make up? Particularly now!'

'No.' Slowly Gabriel shook his dark head. His response was calmer than before, though none of the tension had eased from his long body. 'No, you never lied to me. So he made an honest woman of her at last.'

Rachel winced at the blackly sardonic intonation he gave the words 'an honest woman'. She knew only too well how he felt about Lydia. He had been darkly furious at the way she had, in his eyes at least, invaded his home, usurping his mother's place. So now she could just imagine what ugly thoughts teemed in his suspicious mind. His next comment confirmed as much.

'And was that all?'

'All?' Rachel echoed, not understanding what he was driving at. 'What else could there be?'

Her reply seemed to satisfy him. His smile in response was grimly satirical.

'What else indeed? Lydia must have been over the moon. What was it, a deathbed conversion?'

'They were married in the hospital, yes,' Rachel returned stiffly, hating the sneering way he had framed the question. 'How could it have been anywhere else? After all, your father wasn't exactly capable of a registry office do, let alone a full church wedding.'

That comment had been definitely below the belt, she admitted guiltily, seeing the way his eyes changed. It was as if steel shutters had come down behind them, closing off his thoughts from her.

But it was too late to take it back, however much she wanted to. He hadn't moved, but he had taken several steps away from her, mentally at least, and there was no way she could reach him.

'"Make yourself at home..."'

For a couple of heartbeats Rachel didn't register quite what Gabriel had said. But then, with a painful lurch of her heart, she recognised her own words, flung at him as she'd come back into the room and now mimicked with brutal precision.

'"Make yourself at home, why don't you?"' Gabriel repeated with an ominous emphasis. 'Of course, now I see exactly what you were so churned up about. You'd got your hands on—'

'No!' She saw only too clearly the way his thoughts were heading and hated him for it. 'It was never like that!'

'No?'

That finely carved upper lip curled into a sardonic travesty of a smile, one that was so far from any real warmth that it chilled the blood in her veins.

'Are you trying to claim that your mother never wanted marriage after all? That she never hankered after the respectability my father's name would bring her? And, more than that, that she didn't take one look at this house and want it for her own? It and the money, and the business her husband could leave to her when he died—?'

'No! No, no, no!'

She had to interrupt, to break the flow of those malevolent, cold-voiced accusations.

'You're making it sound so foul, so calculated. Oh, I admit that Mum always wanted marriage. What woman wouldn't dream of a formal commitment to the man she loved?'

It was a struggle not to be put off by his cynical snort of laughter, but she forced herself to ignore it and ploughed on desperately.

'And, yes, she coveted this house. I can't deny that either. But you make it sound as if she took advantage of a dying man. As if she bullied and blackmailed him when he was at his weakest, forcing him into putting a ring on her finger. I swear to you, it wasn't like that!'

Something in what she had said, or simply the vehemence with which she had expressed it, had got through to him. Or perhaps it was the hot tears that only now did she realise were burning in her eyes, preventing her from seeing him clearly.

'What was it like, then?' he asked, his tone so different that she almost gasped in shock.

With an impatient hand she dashed the tears from her eyes, unable to believe that he was actually going to listen to her at last.

'Do you really want to know?'

Another of those curt, decisive nods was his only response, and she drew a long, shuddering breath, clamping down on the emotions he had stirred up. She had to keep calm. She mustn't let him get to her.

'As a matter of fact, they'd planned to get married some time ago. Your father actually proposed on New Year's Day.'

Her face softened as she spoke, a small, reminiscent smile curving the corners of her full mouth.

'He said it seemed an appropriate day for new beginnings.'

What had she said to put that tension back into every muscle in his body? What had there been in her account of the facts to make his jaw clench, make him narrow his eyes in swift, unnerving assessment?

'The wedding was to have been at Easter. They didn't know—' Her voice cracked painfully on the last words. 'They thought they had all the time in the world, and my mother had always dreamed of a spring wedding. She wanted all the trimmings.'

'I'll just bet she did. Don't tell me she was hypocritical enough to go for the white dress and veil for this wedding of the year?'

The sneering tone told her that he still didn't believe her, that deep in that black heart of his the hatred he had always felt towards her mother burned as darkly as before.

'There's no convincing you, is there?' she demanded, and was confronted by yet another of those cold, unfeeling smiles.

'Where your mother is concerned, you'll have to forgive me if I'm not exactly credulous,' he drawled cynically. 'I would need some concrete evidence before you convinced me that...'

If he finished the sentence Rachel didn't hear him as she whirled around, dashing to the elegant bureau that stood in the curve of the large bay window. Hastily pulling open the top drawer, she snatched up a bundle of white cards that lay just inside.

'Here!'

Breathless with urgency, she came back to his side, holding them out to Gabriel.

'Take them!' she urged, pushing them into his hands when he didn't respond, his dark eyes fixed on her face. 'Go on, take them!'

'What's this?' For Gabriel, his reactions seemed

strangely slow. Normally he was always more than one step ahead of everyone.

'The proof you wanted, of course! That "concrete evidence". Look—'

One finger tapped against the cards in his hand, and at last his deep brown gaze dropped to study the wording inscribed in elegant silver script.

'"You are invited to..."' Rachel couldn't endure the silence as he read. '"The wedding of Gregory and Lydia...April fourth..." See? The invitations were printed ready for next month!'

She knew the moment the truth registered from the way his strong fingers clenched on the card, crushing it ruinously.

'They were going to get married anyway!'

'He never told me.'

'Well, why would he? Knowing the way you felt about my mother already, do you think he'd expect you to welcome her into the family?'

It wasn't until she saw how his face whitened that she realised how cruel that had sounded.

'I expect he would have done,' she amended hastily. 'If things had gone as they'd planned. They'd applied for the licence—everything! But they had to bring it forward...'

With the need to convince him no longer sustaining her, she felt all the fight drain out of her suddenly, leaving behind only the black misery she had felt ever since that day. The memory closed her throat, choking her, and her eyes filled with moisture.

'I was their witness.' She gave up her fight to hold back the tears any longer and simply let them cascade freely down her face. 'In the private room. Greg...'

'Oh, God!'

The wedding invitations tumbled to the floor, falling like oversized snowflakes onto the thick piled carpet as Gabriel turned to her. Reaching out, he enfolded her in his arms, drawing her closer with unexpected gentleness.

'Sit down.'

Moving slowly and carefully, he led her to the settee, where he drew her down to sit beside him. One hand came up to slide into the gleaming chestnut hair, cupping the base of her skull and pressing her face close against his shoulder.

'I think I owe you an apology,' he muttered, his voice rough and uneven. 'I should have known you wouldn't lie to me.'

But the careful words offered no balm to the wounds he had inflicted. He might have apologised for not trusting her story of the planned wedding, but he still believed her capable of joining forces with her mother against him. Capable of taking possession of this house that had been his childhood home and holding it against him.

It didn't help to know that she had made the situation worse with her own sarcastic comment.

'I'm sorry,' she choked, lifting tear-filled eyes to his watchful dark ones. 'I should never have said...'

'Shh,' he soothed softly, laying one strong finger across her mouth to silence her.

Rachel's heart beat sharply at the unexpected contact, her mood changing in the space of that heartbeat. She didn't want to feel like this. Didn't want to be so intimately aware of the hard contours of the chest against which her head rested, the controlled strength of the arms that held her.

She wanted to tear herself away and yet knew that any such precipitous action would betray the turmoil of her inner feelings. So she could only freeze, praying that in a moment he would release her and she could break the physical contact that made her whole body tingle as if a surge of electric power had crackled along every nerve.

'Don't blame yourself,' Gabriel continued. 'It's not your fault. It's this damned situation we've found ourselves in. I'm—touchy...'

His mouth twisted at the painful understatement, drawing a shaken laugh from her.

'Oh, God, Gabriel, I should think you're allowed to be "touchy"! You've lost your father, after all, and you didn't even get a chance to say goodbye.'

Shadows deepened the ebony darkness of that steady gaze and all colour suddenly leached from his skin. When she tried to sit up he offered no resistance, his grip loosening apparently without his being aware of it.

With her conscience once more making her feel distinctly uncomfortable, Rachel knew that now was her chance to make up for the careless cruelty of her earlier remarks.

'Would—would you like me to tell you how it...?' she asked shakily, and saw his eyes close briefly, but not before she had caught the unexpected sheen that glimmered on their surface.

He pressed his fingers against the lids for a moment and drew in a deep, painful breath.

But when he opened his eyes again they were clear and calm once more. The ruthless, almost inhuman control she associated with Gabriel, except on one memorable occasion, was once more back in place.

'Would you mind?'

It would be a lie to say no. She did mind. But it was the least she could do.

She might hate him, but she couldn't begin to imagine how she would have felt if their roles had been reversed. If she had been the one summoned by a desperate transatlantic phone call. If she had been told that her father had been involved in a multiple motorway pile-up and was now in Intensive Care.

'In the end, it wasn't the crash that killed him. The doctors told us that his injuries were perfectly treatable. But he'd had a massive heart attack in the ambulance, possibly as a result of the shock. They stabilised him, in fact he seemed to be pulling round, but...'

She shook her head, recalling the horror of that

second, frantic late-night message from the hospital. The phone had been ringing as they'd arrived home, barely an hour after the hastily arranged wedding.

'Perhaps he knew—had some sort of premonition somehow. Because *he* was the one who was so insistent on the marriage being then and there. But he seemed so happy, Gabriel...'

Instinctively she sensed what he needed to know most.

'He was so positive, so sure, and he was never in any pain. They said that when it happened it was so fast that he wouldn't have known a thing. And you were in his mind. He told me to give you his love and tell you that he was proud of what you'd done in America. He—he also said he hoped you'd be able to accept us all as one big family.'

It was only as she finished that she realised she had laced her fingers with Gabriel's own, their joined hands still resting on his knee. Whether she'd done it to comfort him or herself, she couldn't be sure. She only knew that his grip on her hand had tightened, imprisoning hers when she would have eased it away.

'Thank you for that, at least.' It was low-voiced and sombre.

'It was what I would have needed to know.' Still looking down at their linked hands—his, so strong and competent, making hers seem pale and fragile in contrast—she added softly, 'And he knew you were on your way.'

The convulsive movement of those square-tipped fingers over hers betrayed him in a way that his usual rigid control would never let him show. Glancing up swiftly, she locked her concerned gaze with his. Deep, deep pools of burning darkness fixed on her grey eyes and held them.

'Who told him?'

'I did.'

It wasn't an easy admission. She had no idea how he would take it. After all, wasn't it partly because of her mother and the tensions her presence had caused that he had been so far from his father at such a time? Wasn't it because of them that he hadn't seen the older man for more than four years?

'That was kind.'

The evident sincerity of his voice seemed to tangle round her insides, tugging painfully. That sincerity reminded her of a night in the past, of things he had said, declarations he had made, that she had believed, foolishly, naively, blindly.

'I did it for Greg.' It was impossible to control the quaver on the name. 'After all, he meant such a lot to me. He was the only father I ever really had.'

The tears were back again, welling up and spilling out onto her cheeks.

'Rachel—' Gabriel began, but she didn't want him to speak, didn't want him to say something she might not be able to trust and so destroy the fragile peace they had built up between them.

'I never really missed my real dad. After all, at three I was too young to know him properly before he died. So when Greg took us in he didn't *replace* my father. Instead, he filled an empty space in my life, one that had been there so long that I didn't realise how big it had become.'

At sixteen, she had thought that Gabriel too would fill an emptiness in her life. That he would be part of the family she had never had. And, later, she had hoped for so much more. But those dreams had been shattered, shown to be the illusions they were.

'He was so very good to me…'

'He cared about you.'

Something had changed. Gabriel seemed to have stiffened suddenly. The sense of peace she had felt earlier had vanished, and in its place was a new, electric tension, one that unnerved and frightened her.

'Gabriel?'

But as she lifted her swimming eyes to his he made a strange, strangled sound deep in his throat. It was part sigh, part groan. It even seemed to have something that sounded like desperately shaken laughter blended into it.

'Oh, for God's sake, Rachel—come here!'

Perhaps it was the roughness of the way that he pulled her into his arms. Perhaps it was the realisation that here was someone who understood her feelings. Or perhaps it was the sudden overwhelming sense of this being exactly what she needed that broke down any sense of resistance.

Ever since the news of the crash had first broken she had had to be strong for Lydia's sake. She had supported her mother through the long, stress-filled hours, coping with officialdom, handling the necessary formalities as well as the intrusion of the press. There had been no time for her own grief.

But now here was someone strong and capable to help her. Someone into whose hands she could put so much of the responsibility she had struggled with. Someone whose broad shoulders she could rest against and know they would support her.

And so for the first time she succumbed to the misery she had pushed down inside herself. She let it all flow from her in racking sobs, her tears soaking into his immaculate white shirt.

Gabriel simply held her. He didn't say a word, just let her weep. But all the time he held her gently but firmly in his arms, the warmth of his body enclosing her like a protective cocoon. And he waited. Waited until the storm of grief had cried itself out and with a final, gasping sigh her sobs ceased and she lay exhausted against his shoulder.

'Better?' he asked softly, and Rachel could only nod silently.

So much better, she thought privately. How much better she couldn't even begin to tell him. It seemed that in those few brief moments, the space of just a few heartbeats, she had discovered something so very valuable, something vital to her very existence.

She'd got back something of the old Gabriel. The one she had idolised as an adolescent. The man, eight years older than her, she had hero-worshipped from afar and then adored in the throes of her first powerful crush. This was the Gabriel who had been such an essential part of her life from the moment when, at sixteen, she had first moved into Greg Tiernan's house with her mother.

'Much better.' She sniffed inelegantly. 'Thanks.'

'No problem.'

But something was wrong with his voice. The gentle, comforting note had fled, to be replaced by a very different undertone. It was one she was unable to interpret, and it worried her, setting warning bells jangling inside her head.

The change was reflected in the way he held her, in the tautening of every muscle in the powerful body against which she rested. His heartbeat under her cheek was no longer the steady, regular thud of moments before. Instead it was uneven, jerky, betraying a response he was trying to control, a reaction he wanted to hide.

In a moment of shocking, blinding clarity it came to her that it wasn't her reaction he was concerned about but his own. *He* was holding back, fighting the impulse that had driven him to put his arms around her with all his strength.

She was as close to him as it was possible to be, but the rigid restraint Gabriel was imposing on himself meant that they might as well have been at opposite sides of the room.

'Gabriel?'

As she tilted her head to look up into his eyes it was as if a time frame had slid out of joint, putting her life into the wrong sequence. She was back in another day—in another lifetime, it seemed—when she had looked up into that dark gaze and seen what she had believed to be love.

At the time she had fooled herself, convinced herself

that love was what burned there, when all the time it had been a very different, far more basic emotion. It had been nothing other than cold, primitive lust. You could package it up more prettily, disguise it with euphemisms like 'desire' or 'need', but in the end, particularly with this man, it all came down to the same very basic hunger.

But she was no longer the gullible teenager he had once been able to deceive. This time she recognised precisely what she'd seen, and it had an effect like the splash of freezing water right in her face, bringing her back down to earth with a cruel bump. This time she recognised the danger she faced.

What was worse, she also recognised her own part in it, the contribution she had made to putting herself in this situation. Which was all the more devastating because she hadn't even been aware of letting her guard down, of breaking the vow she had made all those years before.

She had promised herself that never again would she let this man hurt her in any way. That armed with hatred she would keep her defences against him in perfect order, with not a single crack, not a chink anywhere that would let his malign influence get through to her.

But—oh, God—something had happened to destroy that certainty. In a moment of weakness she had left herself open to all the forces she had so wished to avoid, and the burning sense of awareness, her instinctively quickened breathing, told their own tale.

'Rachel, are you OK?'

She had been silent too long, arousing his suspicions. In a hasty attempt to cover her tracks she sat up carefully, switching on a smile that felt so insincere she didn't even dare to consider how it must look.

'I'm fine,' she managed, her voice as stiff as her movements.

She didn't want to risk meeting his eyes again, so she put on a pretence of hunting for a handkerchief to mop her tear-stained face. The fact that her handbag was on the opposite side of the room gave her the perfect excuse to get up and move away, which she did thankfully.

After a display of wiping her cheeks and blowing her nose that wouldn't have gone amiss in the worst ever amateur dramatics production, she felt she had collected herself enough to face him again.

'You must want to freshen up, or perhaps have a rest before dinner this evening…'

He hadn't moved. He was still sitting exactly where she had left him, as still and silent as if he had been carved from marble like some ancient Greek statue.

The idea seemed fitting. Gabriel would do justice to the image of some primitive god. That fine, high forehead, the straight nose, those powerfully carved cheekbones, would all look exactly right on a carving of Zeus or Apollo, or perhaps a legendary hero like Theseus or Jason of the Argonauts.

'I think perhaps it's time I showed you to your room.'

Gabriel flexed his shoulders tiredly and ran both hands roughly through the gleaming darkness of his hair. The danger she had sensed in him just moments before seemed to have evaporated, leaving him looking disturbingly vulnerable and, contrary to her fanciful imaginings about Greek gods, all too human.

'I doubt if I could rest,' he said, getting to his feet and stretching slowly. 'I shall just have to wait for the jet lag to catch up with me. But a hot shower would be welcome. I left my bag in the hall…'

'Then Reynolds will have taken it upstairs.'

Rachel had to force the words from a throat that seemed suddenly painfully dry. Telling him about the marriage had only been part of the unpleasant revelations she had to communicate. The second part was coming up at any minute, and she had no doubt he would like it no better than the first.

'Would that be *Mr* Reynolds to the Mrs Reynolds I

met earlier?' The sardonic question jarred on her already overstretched nerves.

'That's right. They both started here just over a year ago.'

'Replacing Mrs Kent and Joe?'

Rachel's head came up defensively in response to the unspoken accusation behind his words.

'They were both getting on a bit, Gabriel. I know how fond of them you were but you've been away a long time. Things change; nothing stands still.'

'So it seems,' was the dry response. 'What next, I wonder?'

Which was enough to put a definite shake into Rachel's legs as she headed for the stairs.

Was it just her own sensitivity, or was he really following her so closely that she felt he was almost breathing down her neck? Did she actually brush against him with every step she took, the tiny hairs on her skin lifting in instinctive reaction?

And yet when she glanced behind her he was a careful, polite distance away, a couple of steps below her. It was just her own sensitivity to his presence, the sense of pins and needles over every inch of her skin, that was making her feel this way.

'Is there really any need for this?' Gabriel asked suddenly as they reached the first landing. 'After all, I know this house even better than you do, seeing as I grew up here. Believe me, I haven't forgotten anything in the last four and a half years. I'm more than capable of finding my own—'

'It isn't yours any more!'

As soon as she had spoken, Rachel cursed her foolishness. How could she have blurted out the truth with such appalling tactlessness? She'd been pushed into it by the sharp twisting of her nerves in response to that 'I haven't forgotten anything'.

Gabriel stopped dead at the top of the stairs, his dark head going back, his eyes narrowing sharply.

'Explain!' he ordered curtly.

Rachel swallowed hard, hunting desperately for the right words and finding none.

'If my room isn't mine any more, then whose—'

'It's mine!' she declared starkly.

He wasn't at all surprised, she realised. It was the answer he had expected all along.

'Oh, how very cosy!' His sarcasm had the bite of acid.

'Your father insisted!'

She knew how much his former room had meant to him when he was younger. It was more of a personal suite or a mini-apartment than just a bedroom. Taking up the whole of the attic floor, it provided a sitting room as well as a tiny *en suite* bathroom, and a door closing off the foot of the stairs up to it ensured complete privacy for its occupant.

And Gabriel had always valued that privacy. In the early days of her life in this house he had taken full advantage of it.

He had made no secret of his hostility towards Lydia, nor of his belief that her affair with his father had been the last straw that had driven his mother away. Because of that, he had spent most of his time up in the attic, only emerging when he had to join the family at meals, and never inviting anyone into his private sanctum.

'Believe me, it wasn't my idea!' she protested. 'He had it completely redecorated as a twenty-first birthday present.'

And no one would ever know how appallingly difficult she had found it to accept the generous present. Not just because it had cost so much, but for other, more personal reasons. The attic would always be linked in her mind with Gabriel, and a night she wished she could forget but knew she never would.

'No, I don't suppose it was.' His drawl was bleakly cynical. 'He always does—did,' he amended with a painful adjustment that seemed to tear a piece out of

Rachel's heart, 'just as he pleased, even if it meant riding roughshod over other people's feelings.'

'He didn't think you were coming back. You made it plain that you thought your future was in America.' She prayed that her voice didn't give any clue as to the personal pain that had caused her too.

'He was probably right,' Gabriel stated flatly. 'I certainly never planned on coming back here until I was married. So tell me, Rachel, dear, if I've been ejected from the attic, then which bedroom have you assigned to me?'

'The blue room.'

It had been a struggle not to choke at that 'until I was married'. She wanted to believe that it was just a throwaway remark, but something about the emphasis he had given the words told her that she couldn't take refuge in any such comfortable retreat.

'Lydia's idea, I presume?'

'No, mine.' She ignored the cynicism lacing the question. 'I—thought you'd be more comfortable there.'

It was the largest bedroom in the house. Bigger even than the one her mother had shared with his father. Perhaps naively, she had hoped that its spacious elegance would go a little way towards compensating for the loss of his old room.

'Comfortable, and at quite the wrong end of the corridor to be a nuisance to you.'

'Nuisance?' She frowned her incomprehension.

'And with Lydia just next door, ready to catch the sound of any suspiciously creaking floorboards.'

His smile, as he saw that she had finally caught the direction of his thoughts, was positively devilish.

'Perhaps it's just as well that the sleeping arrangements will be almost exactly the opposite of when I was last home. We wouldn't want a repeat of past mistakes, would we?'

That wicked smile grew, became even more hateful

in response to the gasp of shock and distress that Rachel was unable to hold back.

'You—'

'But you needn't worry, sweetheart. I have no intention of pouncing on you.'

That 'sweetheart' had the effect of a slap in the face. Anger flared in her eyes, lifting her chin and stiffening her spine.

'I never imagined you had!'

'No? Then what was all that downstairs?'

A wave of his hand indicated the hallway, where the still open door to the sitting room framed the settee on which they had been sitting.

'All what?'

'You know perfectly well what I mean!'

'I was upset!'

'You might have been upset to start with,' he conceded. 'But that soon changed to something else. Then you couldn't wait to get away from me. You leapt up as if you'd just discovered that I had some foul, highly infectious disease, and you felt that just to touch me would contaminate you.'

'You're exaggerating!' Silently she cursed the shake in her voice that betrayed the truth of his analysis and her own unnerved response to it.

'I never exaggerate, Rachel. Never.'

It had all the undertones of an ominous warning, one that stirred the buried memories again, exposing dark, ugly shapes she didn't want to look at too closely.

'But you needn't worry, because I'll tell you something for nothing: your maidenly fears are totally misplaced—no foundation in them at all. You couldn't be safer with a maiden aunt than you are with me.'

'Safe' was not a word that she had ever associated with Gabriel Tiernan, Rachel reflected bitterly. From the moment she had first set eyes on him she had known that he was dangerous, through and through.

He had the sort of dark, ruthless appeal that set

women's nerves on edge, driving them both to want him and to fear him at the same time.

'No?'

Some movement of her head, a tiny change of her expression, must have alerted him to the thoughts that were going through her mind—though, being Gabriel, he put a very different interpretation on her response.

'Believe me, darling.'

His voice was raw with a rough-edged emphasis that cut straight through the defences she was trying to build up against him.

'*Believe me.* Even if I was desperate. If I'd been celibate for a lifetime and a half and I was crawling on my hands and knees with need. Even if I was so burned up with lust that I knew I'd die if I didn't have a woman in my life—in my bed—on this floor, right now. Even then, and if you were the only woman available, the very last woman on earth, I wouldn't touch you!'

He flung out a hand in a violent gesture that had Rachel flinching back against the polished wood of the banisters, fear flaring in her grey eyes.

But Gabriel knew exactly what he was doing, and no part of his body made any sort of contact with hers. Instead, he stilled the movement just in time, snatching his hand back with a speed that was more insulting, more expressive of total rejection, than any words could ever be.

'Then why did you touch me—hold me just now?' It was the cry of a wounded animal. She was past disguising the hurt his words had inflicted on her, even to herself.

His face closed over, even the fury and disgust that had been stamped on his hard features a moment before disappearing under the emotionless mask he now assumed.

'You were hurting and you needed help. Only a mindless brute would have left you to cry on your own. But it will never happen again, Rachel. Stick with the disgust, darling; it's better that way. Because I'll never have anything to do with you like that again. You come *way* too expensive!'

'And what makes you think that you'll ever get the chance even to consider it?' she spat at him, hatred and that disgust he had advised her to feel burning like acid, eating her away inside.

Just for a second Gabriel drew back, seeming to catch his breath sharply. But a moment later he had recovered his fiendishly cool composure.

'You wouldn't like the answer to that one, sweetheart, so don't push me or I might just give it to you. And now, if you don't mind, I really need that shower. If I felt filthy before, it's nothing to the way I feel now!'

Rachel held herself carefully away from him as he came past on the stairs, but there was no need for any such precaution. His own long body was so stiffly distant that there wasn't the remotest chance of them touching.

And she thought she'd got the old Gabriel back! Rachel shook her head despairingly as she watched him walk down the corridor towards his bedroom. What a fool she'd been! What a blind, desperate fool!

There was no *old* Gabriel! There never had been. That had only been a delusion, created by her overactive adolescent imagination, existing only in her fantasies, her pathetic dreams.

This was the true Gabriel, the only Gabriel. Black and foul through and through, as he had proved to be the day after her nineteenth birthday, and nothing about him had changed in the least.

CHAPTER THREE

RACHEL stood at the bottom of the stairs up to the attic, struggling with the fear that had suddenly struck out at her when she had been least prepared for it.

'This is ridiculous!' She said the words out loud to drive them home. 'It can't happen—I won't let it happen! The past is the past; it's over—done with!'

Only it wasn't over, or done with. It had ceased to be over the moment that Gabriel had walked back into the house. And the past wouldn't stay in the past because that single action had flung open a door in her mind, one that she had thought she had locked firmly so long ago.

But it hadn't stayed locked. And, like Pandora with her box, opening it had released into her life all that was foul and hateful, polluting the peace she thought she'd gained.

In the hall below, a door opened and closed again, and the sound of heavy, masculine footsteps came up the stairs, pushing her into hasty action. She didn't want Gabriel to catch her here like this.

Dinner had been over for a couple of hours. An unbearably long-drawn-out meal, every second of it had seemed like an endurance test.

She had been supremely conscious of Gabriel sitting directly opposite her on the far side of the highly polished table, another of those immaculate suits and a fresh shirt and tie testimony to his respect for the rule made long ago by his father that 'In this house we dress for dinner'.

'"I'll have none of that casual slobbing about that everyone seems to be going in for these days,"' Gabriel had quoted drily when she had joined him before the meal. 'You see? He still rules our lives even when he's gone.'

'Your father always liked things done with style.'

'And he liked to see beautiful women elegantly dressed,' Gabriel had returned, his dark gaze skimming over her deep purple velvet dress.

The gaze had been cool and controlled, and there was no trace of the disturbing fires she had seen in his eyes earlier. But all the same he had made her shiveringly aware of the way the rich fabric smoothed over the lines of her body, emphasising the curves of breasts and hips. It might be long-sleeved and high-necked, but it had a subtle sensuality that made her wish she had chosen something less clinging.

'He would definitely have approved of the way you've followed his instructions. Is the jewellery your own work?'

'These?'

Rachel had touched the silver and amethyst earrings with fingers that shook faintly, grateful for an excuse to distract that ebony gaze upwards and away from her body. Once again she'd been a prey to that sensation of having a layer of skin scraped away, so that even the soft velvet she wore had tantalised every nerve-end with excruciating sensitivity.

'Yes, I made them. Greg gave me the stones last Christmas, and I planned the design around them.'

Another generous present from his father. Would he react to that as he had to the news that she had been given the attic room? But Gabriel had simply nodded, sipping his drink slowly.

'They're spectacular,' he'd said easily. 'You're very talented.'

That had been the nearest they'd come to anything that could remotely be termed real conversation. Her mother had joined them at that moment, and as soon as she'd walked into the room the atmosphere, hardly particularly warm to start with, had become what could only be described as icy. Such comments as passed between them had been stilted, formally polite. They'd stuck strictly to neutral, uncontentious topics while struggling with a meal that no one had seemed to have any appetite for.

As soon as she could, Lydia had given up even pretending to eat. She had made hasty excuses and retired to her bedroom before the dessert was served. Rachel and Gabriel had soldiered on for a short time before he'd pushed his half-full plate away from him, tossing his linen napkin onto the table.

'I must be more jet lagged than I thought. I shall have to make my apologies to Mrs Reynolds in the morning.'

'I'm sure she'll understand.'

She was grateful for the chance to stop picking at her food herself, and pushed back her chair with a sigh of relief.

'No one's exactly in a mood to appreciate her cooking these days. Coffee?'

'I'll leave it, if you don't mind. I wouldn't want to risk the caffeine interfering with a good night's sleep. But I'll have a brandy, if I may.'

'Of course. You don't have to ask, this is…'

The words died on her lips, shrivelled up by the searing look he threw her. It wasn't his home any longer, it said without words, and she damn well knew it.

'Help yourself,' she said crisply. 'But forgive me if I don't join you. It's been a long day, so I'll just check on Mum and go on up.'

She changed out of the velvet dress first, removing her make-up and slipping on a cream rose-patterned silky robe before knocking softly on her mother's door.

To her surprise Lydia was inclined to talk, and so kept her much longer than she anticipated. It was as she crossed the darkened landing on her way back to her own room that the panic attack struck, freezing her fingers on the door handle.

She couldn't go up to the attic. There were too many memories linked with those rooms, too close to the surface of her mind.

But now she was terrified that Gabriel would reach the top of the stairs and see her standing there, shocked into immobility like a rabbit caught in the headlights of an oncoming car. With an urgent shake of her head she ordered herself to snap out of her trance and open the door. Slipping onto the staircase behind it, she pulled it to behind her quickly.

She was only just in time. Her heart was still beating frantically as she heard Gabriel reach the landing and head down the corridor towards his own room. As he moved further away, past her mother's door, the faint creak of an uneven floorboard brought his cruel comments earlier swiftly to mind.

'We wouldn't want a repeat of past mistakes…'

If only *she* had been deterred by the thought of her mother hearing a floorboard creak, Rachel thought miserably, forcing her unwilling feet up the stairs again. Then perhaps things would never have gone as far as they had that night. But Greg and her mother had been out at the theatre, and she and Gabriel had had the house to themselves.

It was something of a shock when she finally reached her bedroom and switched on the light to be confronted by the feminine peach and cream colour scheme her mother had chosen for her when the attic had been redecorated.

She had almost believed that she would find it restored to the dark green and bronze uncompromisingly masculine decor Gabriel had favoured. That was how she had seen it first and how she would always imagine it in the privacy of her thoughts.

Not that she had been honoured with an invitation up to his private sanctum when she had first arrived at the house. For a long time Gabriel had been so hostile to

Lydia's presence that he had kept his distance, both physical and mental, from them.

But then slowly, gradually, he had started to come round. He had actually begun to talk to Rachel, moved on to a teasing tolerance, and in the end—or so she had believed—had displayed something close to affection for her.

Rachel herself had been knocked for six when she had first encountered Greg's tall, dark and devastating son. She had never met anyone like him, and, fresh from university, working with his father's international jewellery company, he had seemed impossibly sophisticated to her sixteen-year-old eyes.

Such conversations as they'd had had inevitably been brief and awkward, with Rachel stumbling over her words, barely able to form coherent sentences, she was so overawed. She could still recall precisely the day, eighteen months later, when it had changed.

It had been Gabriel's birthday and she had summoned up the courage to ask him how old he was. His reply had surprised her.

'Twenty-six? But you only left university two years ago. What happened? Did you have to resit your exams?'

As soon as she heard her own words she wished that the ground would open up and swallow her. But Gabriel seemed to be in a mellow mood, and he actually laughed.

'You don't exactly flatter my ego, do you?' he drawled. 'But, no, there is a less embarrassing explanation for my late graduation. I took a couple of years out between sixth form and university. Did voluntary work in Africa.'

He named a country still riven by civil war and struggling with a desperate refugee crisis. Rachel had seen appalling pictures of it on the television only the night before, and it sent a cold shiver down her spine to think of him out there in those terrible conditions.

'But wasn't it horrendous? How did you put up with it?'

'It was tough,' Gabriel returned laconically. 'But, as to putting up with it, once you're there you can't think about that, let alone think twice. You and I have an alternative, but those people don't have any choice. They *have* to endure the conditions because there's nothing else, and when you recognise that you see that you can cope with anything for the short time you're there.'

'What made you decide to do it?' Rachel didn't even try to hide the awestruck admiration in her voice.

'A bad case of guilty conscience,' was the wry response. Getting to his feet in a restless movement, he paced to the window to stand staring out at the view of the river Thames that could just be seen in the distance.

'I was young, healthy, no ties, and I'd had a remarkably privileged upbringing. I suddenly realised that I was on a conveyor belt—an extremely comfortable, fur-lined conveyor belt—from school to university to a job with my father, eventually taking over the family business. I wanted to stop it and get off before it all became too easy, before I grew accustomed to it. I wanted to do something worthwhile.'

'You don't consider Tiernan's worthwhile?'

The question brought him swinging round. 'Creating exclusive jewellery for the very rich? It's hardly world-shattering, is it?'

'But I'd love to do something like that! And if it makes you very rich, as it has made your father, then think of what you could do with the money—buy food, build hospitals. If I had a fortune that's how I'd spend it. You could do so much!'

'How true.'

The murmured comment seemed to be threaded through with a satirical note that stung sharply, making her turn wide, reproachful grey eyes on his saturnine face.

'There's no need to mock me! I know you think I'm hopelessly naive and stupid...'

'Never that!' Gabriel interrupted sharply. 'Believe me, sweet Rachel, I could never consider you *stupid.* Innocent, perhaps. Vulnerable—and, yes, rather naive.'

'I'm not a baby!' Rachel's soft lips formed a protesting pout. 'I'll be eighteen next week!'

'But you are still young enough to believe totally in your ideals. Unfortunately, little one, real life isn't like that; it's much more complicated.'

As he spoke Gabriel came back across the room, perching himself on the arm of her chair, looking down into her smoky eyes.

'For one thing there are problems in the world beside which every penny of the money I could earn in my lifetime would seem like just a drop in the ocean. Sometimes all we do is just shore up the defences until such time as they're breached once more and it all starts again.'

He sighed deeply, pushing both hands through his hair as he looked round at the luxurious room with its elegant furnishings.

'Money has a nasty habit of making you forget what's really important in life. Before you know it you're addicted to what it can buy, and from then on however much you have it's never enough. You want another—bigger—better. A new car, a new house...'

A distinct pause. A swift, assessing glance at her upturned face.

'A new wife?' Rachel inserted when he appeared to have decided against saying it. 'Well, a new lover anyway,' she amended, knowing that, legally at least, his father was still married to his mother.

As Gabriel nodded silently she found herself thinking back, counting years. If Gabriel had gone to Africa straight from the sixth form, then...

'Was that another part of the reason you decided to

take time out?' she asked hesitantly, afraid of treading on too many toes.

She guessed that Lydia hadn't been the only 'other woman' in Greg's life. And she knew that her mother had first met him over twenty years before, but she assumed their affair had been very brief, a volatile relationship that had broken up almost as soon as it had started, because very soon afterwards Lydia had met John Amis and married him.

'Because I found out my father was unfaithful to my mother?' Gabriel finished for her when she couldn't complete the question. 'It had a lot to do with it. When what you've always believed are the foundations of your life crumble beneath your feet you start to question everything else as well—even what you most dreamed of doing all your life. So I put university on hold and went off to find myself.'

The dark flippancy of his tone was disturbing, making Rachel shift uncomfortably in her chair.

'And did you manage it?'

'I came back, didn't I?'

Gabriel's smile twisted something painfully in her stomach.

'Thought I'd got my head round things. I even believed my parents had called a halt to hostilities. It was barely six months before I realised it was only an armed truce and my father was up to his old tricks again.'

Abruptly he got to his feet again, shaking his head at his memories as he pushed his hands deep into the pockets of his jeans, broad shoulders slightly hunched.

'I don't believe this,' she heard him mutter.

'Don't believe what? *What*?' she pressed when he simply stared at her, obviously in two minds as to whether to continue. 'Gabriel!'

Briefly he shrugged, as if dismissing his own doubts, watching her all the time with dark, impenetrable eyes.

'I can't believe I'm telling you all this—that I'm discussing such things with a child.'

After the way he had confided in her, the delight she had felt at being treated as someone worth bothering with, someone whose opinions mattered, his sudden reversal to the lofty condescension he had used in the past hurt terribly. She felt as if she had just been slammed hard up against a solid brick wall.

'I'm not a *child*!' It was impossible to erase the pain from her voice. 'And I'm not totally ignorant of life, you know! I may only have been tiny when it happened, but I remember how it felt when my father died, the struggle to understand that he was *never* coming back, the fear that perhaps my mother, and everyone else that I loved…'

'Oh, God, I'm sorry!'

With a swift movement Gabriel came back to her, dropping down onto the arm of the chair once more. One strong hand came gently under her chin, lifting her face so that he could look deep into her eyes. She heard him curse savagely under his breath as he caught sight of the sheen of tears turning her eyes to silver.

'I didn't think! I'm sorry.'

Rachel dashed away the tears with the back of her hand and tried to look suitably defiant.

'I do know—'

'I believe you do,' he assured her deeply. 'After all, you're such a solemn, serious little thing.'

Gentle fingers smoothed a strand of bright hair away from her face, tucking it behind her ear with a tenderness that made her heart thud painfully. His eyes were so deep and dark that she felt she might almost drown in them.

Was he going to kiss her? She desperately wished that he would. It would be all she had ever dreamed of, what she wanted most in all the world.

'I…'

But she never learned what Gabriel had been about to say, or do, because in that moment the door opened sharply.

'So this is where you are!'

Lydia's grey eyes took in the scene before her in one swift, assessing glance, the frown that drew her carefully shaped brows together making it plain that she did not approve in the least.

'Rachel! I told you to go to your room and do your homework! What are you doing hanging around here...?'

It took a moment for her daughter to recover from the jolting shock of her arrival. Gabriel, however, seemed perfectly composed, though he eased his hand away from her cheek with a slow care that Rachel longed to interpret as reluctance to break the gentle contact.

'I...' she tried to protest.

'Upstairs now!'

Rachel's eyes went to Gabriel's face, seeking his support, but he only smiled commiseratingly and jerked his head in the direction of the doorway.

'Better do as you're told. After all, you're never going to make that fortune you talked of if you neglect your schoolwork.'

With a mutinous sigh she got to her feet and stomped from the room. She had just reached the stairs when she heard her mother's voice again, drifting through the partially opened door, the hostility in it clear for anyone to hear.

'I'll thank you to leave my daughter alone, Gabriel! She's a fanciful child, and I don't want you filling her head with any nonsense...'

'You needn't worry, Mrs Amis,' Gabriel cut in with the stiff formality that shaded every word he addressed to Lydia. 'Whatever evil designs you suspect me of having towards Rachel exist only inside your head. I can assure you that I think of her only as a young friend, and as such she couldn't be safer with me.'

The glow of excited hope that had flared so briefly inside Rachel, heating her blood and making her heart race, evaporated so rapidly that she felt shivery and sick, as if in the grip of some virus. She didn't want to be *safe* with Gabriel! And the very last thing she wanted was for him to regard her as a young *friend*!

Coming back to the present with a jolt, Rachel was stunned to find that she had been sitting on the edge of her bed, staring into space while memories played inside her head like some film projected on the screen of her thoughts.

She hadn't even put on the light, and the darkness and silence of the night hung round her like a bleak, suffocating cloak. Even the heating had gone off, the chill of an early spring night filling the room.

With a convulsive shiver she got to her feet, rubbing her arms to warm herself as she tried to shake off the hold the past had on her. Her first thought was to snap on the light, but even its sudden glare couldn't drive away the shadows that still lingered. They clung to the corners of her mind like thick, sticky cobwebs, clouding her thoughts.

If only things could have stayed the way they'd been that day. If only she had left well enough alone. That way she might have stayed as safe as Gabriel had declared her to be.

But her burgeoning sexuality, her female pride, had been piqued by the things she had overheard. She had seen them in the light of a challenge, rather than as a final statement of intent.

Or at least she had felt like that later. At first she had dashed upstairs to her bedroom, flinging herself on her bed where she had wept uncontrollably, pounding the pillow with her clenched fists.

In the end she'd had no tears left, and lay as her gasping breaths gradually slowed, her thoughts centring on the moment that Gabriel had touched her face.

'He *wanted* to kiss me! I know he did!' she'd told herself. 'And he would have done if *she* hadn't come in!'

And he had only said those awful things to please her mother. He had never meant any of them.

She almost convinced herself. But in the end what Gabriel had actually felt or what he hadn't wasn't exactly part of the equation. *She* loved *him*, and she was determined that one day he would know the way she felt about him.

One day, she had vowed, he would notice her for real. He would recognise her as an adult, a mature woman, and she would make sure that he would never, ever see her as anything remotely resembling a child or feel anything as simple as mere friendship towards her ever again.

She'd meant every word of those vows, Rachel recalled miserably. She'd acted on them as devoutly as if they had been sworn on a bible in a court of law. And as a result from that moment on she had never been anywhere near *safe* with Gabriel ever again.

CHAPTER FOUR

'THE waiting is always the worst, isn't it?'

'I'm sorry?'

Startled, Rachel swung round from where she had been staring sightlessly out of the sitting-room window to find Gabriel standing close behind her. He had come into the room, silent as a cat on the thick green carpet, while she had been absorbed in her own thoughts.

At last what he had said began to dawn on her.

'Oh, yes.'

The waiting is always the worst.

'That was what you always used to say to reassure me if I was scared at the thought of an exam, or going to the dentist.'

'Which you hated,' Gabriel said with a faint smile.

'Still do.'

The way that smile grew in response to her exaggerated shudder caught on her nerves and tugged at them sharply.

With her late-night thoughts and even later dreams of the younger, more approachable Gabriel lingering in her mind, it took a moment or two for her to recognise him as the man who stood before her now.

Dark-suited, sombre-faced, his eyes looked shadowed—as if, like her, he had endured an uneasy night. But she was sure that if he had it would have been for none of the same reasons.

'You said the waiting for something was the worst because once you've actually started you're already that much closer to having it over and done with than you were before. And you were usually right.'

'Usually?'

'Well, this time I'm not sure that I want to begin, because once the funeral is over there will be nothing more I can do for Greg.'

'That's the hard part, isn't it?' Gabriel agreed bleakly. 'When you finally have to let go. How's your mother bearing up?'

Seeing the flash of surprise in her eyes, he frowned darkly.

'Oh, don't look so threatened, Rachel! I'm not totally inhuman so that I can't sympathise with what she's going through. And I did sleep in the bedroom next to hers last night.'

And if her mother had cried herself to sleep, as she had ever since the accident, then he would have had to be deaf not to hear it.

'She's calmer this morning,' she told him. 'I think she feels better for having something to do. I promised I'd fetch her when the cars arrived, but I needed a little time to myself first.'

'I know exactly how you feel.'

As Gabriel nodded understanding, the sudden jolt of her heart in response to the rare moment of unity had her hunting for something to say that was less emotive. She found it in the fact that he had just come back into the room after answering the telephone.

'Was that your mother?' She had learned only the night before that Gabriel's mother now lived in Australia, where she had moved after the break-up of her marriage.

'Yes. She wanted to let me know she was thinking of us all this morning.'

'That's kind of her.' It was impossible not to show her surprise at that 'all'.

Gabriel understood exactly what was in her mind.

'My mother feels no resentment towards you or your mother, Rachel. What happened was seven years ago, and she always knew what Greg was like. That's why, in spite of everything, she's sorry not to be here. She would have been if she hadn't had that fall.'

'But no one could expect her to come all the way from Australia with a broken ankle. It's a pity, though. I would have liked to meet her.'

'She feels exactly the same.'

There was a strangely edgy undertone to Gabriel's words as his eyes moved over the simple, almost severe lines of the plain black dress she wore.

'I'm sure she'd be impressed if she saw you now. You look very—elegant.' His tone took the description to a point several miles away from complimentary. 'No jewellery today?'

Automatically Rachel's hands lifted to her unadorned neck. 'I didn't think it appropriate.'

The word made his mouth twist wryly.

'*Appropriate*. My father's favourite definition—well, one of them. But how could it be inappropriate to wear wonderful jewellery to a jeweller's funeral? Besides, you know how Dad always hated black. He said it was a morbid colour and its only redeeming feature was that it was a wonderful background to the necklaces and brooches he created—setting them off to perfection. You should wear something he loved.'

'Are you sure?'

It was what she had originally thought of doing, but in the end she hadn't dared to go with her instinct. There would be so many people at the funeral: Greg's friends, business associates, prestigious customers. She hadn't wanted to put her foot in it by doing something they would consider in bad taste.

'Positive. Go on...'

Firm hands closed over her shoulders, turning her towards the door, a gentle push setting her on her way.

'Go back upstairs and choose something truly spectacular. Wear it with pride—for him.'

Later, Rachel was to wonder whether Gabriel's suggestion had been a deliberate ploy to distract her, to fill in the long, empty moments of waiting that she had been dreading. If it had, then it worked perfectly.

By the time she had selected the jewellery she wanted and put it on, the funeral cars were already at the door. She barely had time to pull on her coat and cram a hat over the burnished colour of her hair before taking her mother's arm as they headed for the door.

It was only when she caught sight of the hearse standing waiting on the driveway that a new and very disturbing thought struck her. This was the first time that Gabriel had been confronted by the stark reality of his personal loss. She turned sharply, and her eyes sought his.

He looked so pale that it seemed a miracle he was still standing so proudly upright. Those dark eyes were more black than brown, sheened with a betraying brightness that she recognised only too painfully.

'Gabriel...'

Impulsively she held out her hand to him.

For the space of several heartbeats her breath caught in her throat as she saw him hesitate, and she nerved herself for the pain his rejection of her spontaneous gesture would bring. But then her fingers were taken in a grip that had neither the warmth of feeling nor the rigid control of distance but was somehow a blend of the two. With her mother still clinging to the other hand, they walked to the car together.

By the time they arrived at the church, Gabriel appeared to be back in control. His stiff-faced silence throughout the journey had led Rachel to believe that he had drawn in on himself, and so she was genuinely surprised to see how, once he was out of the car, he moved to her mother's side, offering her his arm for support.

She was even more astounded by the way her mother accepted, after only a brief hesitation, even managing a faint smile of thanks. A moment later Gabriel turned to her too, long fingers closing around her elbow to draw her nearer.

She took his arm, grateful for its comfort, the feel of its strength under her hand. And suddenly she found that his gesture had taken on such significance that in spite of the sorrow of the occasion it was as if some fragile ray of sun had slipped through the clouds for a moment, lifting her heart in response.

Gabriel was at her side throughout the service, for the burial itself, and again when they finally returned to the house for the formal wake.

'If I could have spared you this, I would have done,' he murmured, coming up behind her as she hesitated in the doorway, drawing in a deep, calming breath, nerving herself to face what seemed to her to be a huge crowd of people. 'But someone has to act as hostess, and your mother clearly couldn't take any more so I sent her upstairs to lie down.'

'Perhaps I should…'

Rachel half turned towards the stairs, only to find herself caught and swung back. For the second time that day firm hands closed over her shoulders, but this time they exerted considerably more force. Hard fingers bit into her tender flesh through the fine wool of her dress.

'Oh, no, you don't,' he declared harshly. 'Mrs Reynolds has taken her a tray of tea and one of the tablets the doctor prescribed. She'll look in on her from time to time, so you're not needed there. You aren't going to chicken out of this—'

'*Chicken out*!' The words escaped in a snap of fury through tightly clenched teeth. 'I was doing no such thing!'

Her head came up, shoulders straightening, grey eyes blazing like diamonds above the new wash of colour in her cheeks. Shaking off his controlling hands, she marched into the room, a careful, social smile plastered firmly onto her face.

It was perhaps twenty minutes later, as she caught the way those watchful brown eyes were fixed on her face and saw his faint, approving nod as her gaze clashed with his, that it occurred to her to wonder if she had been carefully outmanoeuvred once again.

Just as he had sent her upstairs to put on the jewellery that morning, so now he had dealt coolly and calmly with the panic that had almost overwhelmed her on their return to the house. Her apprehension must have been stamped on her face only too clearly, and Gabriel had seen it and acted promptly to help.

'All right?'

He was at her side again—from nowhere, it seemed. In his hands were two glasses of white wine, one of which he held out to her.

'I reckon you deserve this.'

But Rachel wasn't listening, was concentrating instead on his question.

'Of course I'm all right! But then you knew that I would be if you provoked me enough.'

It was only when her retort made the corners of his mouth curl into the first genuine smile she'd seen on his face all day that she realised just how much the funeral had taken out of him.

For all that he moved amongst their guests with an easy charm, with a word for everyone, recalling every name and some personal detail with a flattering accuracy, there was an emptiness about his eyes that told its own story. His sorrow followed him like a shadow, seeming to dim his normally brilliant personality in a way that tore at her heart.

'You just needed a push,' he told her, with another, slightly wider smile. 'But I don't know why you were so scared. You can handle a select gathering—a few friends...'

'A few friends! Gabriel, it's more than that and you know it.'

Rachel indicated the crowded room with the hand that held her glass, her still jittery state of mind revealed in the wildness of a gesture that threatened to send wine over Gabriel's expensively tailored suit.

'There are so many people here from the world of big business—international names most of them. And then there are your dad's customers—they *have* to be out of the top drawer if they could afford his prices. I'm sure I've even seen a couple of minor royals. It might be what *you* term a select gathering, but I don't belong here. I mean, no matter how much I loved Greg, to everyone here I'm simply his mistress's daughter.'

She'd said something wrong there. Very wrong. Something that narrowed his mouth, tightened the muscles in his jaw. His fingers clenched over the stem of the glass he held until she feared it might actually shatter in his hand.

'His *widow's* daughter,' he corrected tautly after a moment's nerve-stretching silence.

Of course. That was where she'd put her foot in it. He hadn't liked Lydia living here as Greg's mistress, seeing it as an insult to his mother. He liked it even less now that she was there as the second Mrs Tiernan.

Or did he? Could the man who had shown her mother such courteous consideration all day still hold onto the bitter hostility he had felt towards her at first?

'They don't know about the wedding yet,' she muttered in a raw undertone. Matters were made all the more difficult by the need to ensure that her words weren't heard by anyone standing nearby. 'We haven't exactly made a public announcement.'

'They'll know soon enough,' he shot back. 'Once the will is read tomorrow, no one will be in any doubt as to the truth of the situation. If this marriage is legal...'

'If!'

Rachel's anger drove her to forget any concern for propriety, her unwisely raised voice drawing several sharp glances that had her hastily adjusting her tone.

'What do you mean *if* it's legal?' she demanded, the ferocity of her response in no way affected by the need to keep its volume low. 'Of course it is! I'll have you know—'

'Then all the more reason for you to meet as many people as you can, show them you appreciate their coming,' Gabriel inserted smoothly, defusing her anger by the simple expedient of refusing to rise to it. 'Don't worry, I'll back you up. Come with me and I'll introduce you...'

He moved off into the crowd again, not even glancing back to see if she was following. Clearly he took her acquiescence for granted.

And he had good cause to, Rachel admitted crossly. Short of making a very awkward and embarrassing scene, she had no option but to follow him. Switching on her social smile once more, she set off determinedly in Gabriel's wake.

It seemed to take for ever until the last guest had finally departed and the house was silent once again. Even with Gabriel at her side—and true to his word he had never left it for a second—the afternoon had been an ordeal she was glad to see the end of. She was deeply thankful to close the door behind the last person to leave.

'Thank God that's over!'

Gabriel's voice echoed her feelings as he shrugged himself out of his superbly fitted jacket, tossing it carelessly onto a nearby chair. Flinging himself down on the settee, he pushed his hands through his hair with a deep sigh of relief. The dark silk tie was tugged loose at his throat, following the jacket a moment later to lie coiled like a sloughed-off snakeskin over the blue cushions.

'I really have nothing in common with some of Dad's clients—or his friends! Making conversation with them is one hell of an effort. Today was an ordeal I wouldn't care to have to repeat.'

And yet he'd thought that *she* should go through that ordeal with him, Rachel thought, irritation flaring at the recollection of the way he had pushed her into it. If he had had enough, then she had had twice that.

'But at least we've done our duty. Where the hell are you going?'

Rubbed raw by the curtness of his question, Rachel swung round sharply.

'To see how my mother is. She's been alone...'

'She's fine. Mrs Reynolds checked on her a few minutes ago and found her sound asleep. From the way she looked this morning, I should imagine she'll sleep the clock round now she's finally drifted off. It'll do her the world of good. So you've no need to worry. You can just relax.'

Relax! Just in time Rachel caught back a snort of cynical laughter. She was worn out, longed to be in bed and asleep like her mother, and the thought of being alone with Gabriel almost made her wish that some of the afternoon's guests would come back.

'I thought we could have some tea—sit down, Rachel,' he cajoled, when she hovered between the settee and the door. 'I promise I won't bite!'

The thought of tea was tempting, Rachel admitted privately, moving back into the room with a show of reluctance. But if he said one thing out of place, made one more snide remark casting doubt on the legality of her mother's marriage, then she'd empty the teapot, leaves and all, right over that glossy dark head.

She gave a grim little smile at the thought of what that would do to the expensive white shirt that somehow managed to look as fresh now, at the end of a long day, as it had when he had first put it on.

'Besides, I think we need to talk.'

'Do we?' Rachel asked warily, fixing her attention on the tray that the housekeeper had placed on a table beside her. Concentrating on pouring the tea as if her life depended on not spilling a single drop, she added, 'Talk about what?'

'About how extremely talented you are, for one,' Gabriel stunned her by replying. 'I love that necklet you're wearing. I take it it is one of your designs? That cup's full!'

'Of course it's one of mine!'

Rachel knew that in slamming the teapot down she was reacting to something more than the undercurrent of laughter in his gentle warning that she was about to let the tea spill over. Something that went far deeper and affected her much more than his compliment on her work.

There was something in the way that he looked at her. Something that turned the deep brown of his eyes to burning onyx in the same moment that it set the tiny hairs on the back of her neck lifting in tingling awareness. She was uncomfortably conscious of a pulse throbbing at the base of her throat, the suddenly accelerated beat of her heart making her breasts rise and fall with her uneven breathing.

'I wouldn't wear anything else, today of all days.'

'I realise that. It's just that I can't see Dad being willing to sell something as dramatic—almost primitive—as that, unless it was for a special one-off commission.'

'No, you're right,' Rachel admitted, a smile slipping past her guard. 'He would never do that.'

Grow up! she told herself, with a brusque mental shake. She was overreacting, behaving as she had done all those years ago when as an overawed adolescent she hadn't been able to sit still in his presence. She didn't feel like that any more.

She would have preferred the words to have had more conviction inside her head. But even as she thought them it was impossible not to recall the electric current of awareness that had burned through her so many times that afternoon simply because his hand had brushed hers, or his breath had warmed her cheek as he'd murmured yet another name in her ear.

'The things I make for myself to wear are not the sort of things I design for Tiernan's. Greg's customers are every bit as conventional—almost old-fashioned—as ever. They want quality stones and the finest gold and silver, but in very traditional settings. Occasionally...'

It was a heartfelt sigh of regret.

'Just occasionally I get a chance to do something a little different, something that stretches me, but not often.'

Seeing the way he nodded, the empathic understanding she could read in his face, she suddenly felt so close to him that it was almost more than she could bear.

'Wasn't that the reason why you and he argued?' she asked impulsively. 'The reason you went off to America to set up on your own?'

'Partially,' he returned carefully, looking down into his cup as if it held some secret message. 'There were other reasons.'

She would have liked to ask more, but, getting the distinct impression that she was being warned off, decided to play it safe instead.

'But, like me, you always wanted to make Tiernan's more adventurous. Like those African designs you showed me once.'

It had been perhaps five days or so after her mother had interrupted them on his birthday. She had asked Gabriel some further question about Africa, and their conversation had led him to get out his photographs of his time there.

At first she had used the occasion simply as an excuse to spend more time with him, enjoy his attention. But very soon she had seen why he had fallen in love with the country, and had become totally absorbed. When he had shown her examples of the native jewellery she had been entranced, excited and finally inspired.

'I couldn't believe my eyes; I thought they were wonderful. I'd never seen anything like them in my life before. That was when I made up my mind to become a jewellery designer if I could.'

She had even confided her ambition to Gabriel, blushing shyly, expecting him to laugh. Instead, he had been generously encouraging.

'My father always said he knew you'd be an original,' Gabriel put in now. 'He told me that he once saw you playing with modelling clay, when you were perhaps five or six, and he knew then that—'

'He knew *then*!' Rachel could hardly believe what he'd said. 'I didn't know he'd seen me when I was so small. Mum never said.'

'It certainly wasn't something he broadcasted.' Gabriel's mouth twisted on the words. 'Certainly my mother and I had no idea of Lydia's existence—or yours—until seven years ago.'

He was replacing his cup on the tray, taking almost excessive care about positioning it safely.

'But it seems he knew you both well before that. What sort of things are you working on now?' he continued, with an obvious change of subject. 'Anything as unusual as that necklet?'

'I've been thinking of some bracelets. Very stark, very plain, but gloriously dramatic.' Rachel's instinctive enthusiasm for her subject clashed with her attempt to work out exactly what he was trying to distract her from. 'One or two of them have come out just as I want them.'

'Have you got your designs here, or did you leave them at the office?'

'They're upstairs, in my studio. Would you like to see them?'

'I would—very much. Why don't you fetch them down while I see about some fresh tea?'

His interest was so obviously sincere that Rachel's feet almost danced up the stairs to the attic. This was exactly how it had felt to have her adored Gabriel's attention and interest when she was younger. It hadn't often happened, but then a mature and sophisticated twenty-six-year-old had obviously found little to interest him in her school activities. But things had changed when she had gone on to art college.

For one thing she had no longer been forced to wear the old-fashioned and unflattering school uniform, but could choose whatever she liked. And with Greg's generous allowance providing more money than she had ever had in her life before, she'd been able to indulge her taste for the simple but dramatic styles in wonderful fabrics that she had always yearned for but never been able to afford before then.

Her neat, short schoolgirl's hairstyle had been abandoned too. Instead she had let the bronze coloured locks grow down past her shoulders, discovering to her surprise that they had a wayward tendency to fall into natural waves.

From a couple of comments that Gabriel had made, and a light she had sometimes seen in those black-coffee-coloured eyes, she had known that at last he was beginning to see her more as an adult, a woman, rather than as a mere child. But that had been all. There had been other women in his life, older, sleeker, expensively stylish women, who'd been replaced with an almost frightening regularity—sometimes even before she'd had time to learn their names, let alone regard them as serious rivals.

But at the Christmas after her eighteenth birthday she had manoeuvred herself and Gabriel under the mistletoe, claiming the traditional kiss as hers by right.

For one dreadful moment, seeing him hesitate, she'd thought he was going to refuse, but at last he'd shrugged his shoulders resignedly.

'On your own head be it!' he laughed, lowering his mouth to hers.

It started off as a gentle, almost jokey kiss, and she was sure that that was all he intended. But in the first second that their lips touched it was as if a switch had been thrown, setting a powerful current blazing through every cell, every nerve in her body.

If the air around them had actually crackled with electricity she wouldn't have been surprised. Every inch of skin was pulsing with heat; she was straining towards him, needing to feel his lean, hard strength against her.

And to her blissful amazement Gabriel too seemed to feel the effect of that first stunning, zinging contact. He changed his approach, taking instead just tiny, tormentingly brief kisses that were only enough to tantalise, to arouse, to create hunger without offering any appeasement.

When she moaned a protest he laughed deep in his throat. That laughter died on a raw, choking sound when she took the initiative herself, crushing her mouth against his, opening her lips so that her tongue could tangle with his. Her pulse had danced along her veins as she felt him respond, penetrate her inner softness, tasting her fully.

'Rachel!'

Her name was a shaken sound she found impossible to interpret.

Gabriel fastened his hands over her arms, putting her away from him as his head came up. The struggle he was obviously having to control his disordered breathing left him speechless for a short time.

'Sweetheart,' he managed at last, 'I think this has gone quite far enough. You don't know what you're doing, what you're inviting...'

'Of course I do!' she protested.

Newly intoxicated with an awareness of herself as a woman, feeling instinctively the power her female sexuality gave her, she took the necessary couple of steps back towards him.

Deliberately she slid her tongue out and along her top lip, where the taste of his kiss still lingered, her excitement growing as she saw his eyes drop to watch the small movement.

'Gabriel...'

But at that moment the telephone shrilled loudly, breaking into the silence with a shattering suddenness.

'Ignore it!' she pleaded as his head turned in the direction of the sound. 'Please, don't answer it!'

'Rachel, believe me, it would be a much better idea if I did. For one thing your mother and my father will be home at any moment, and for another you're still so very young. I am not in the habit of cradle-snatching, however tempting the baby!'

Cradle-snatching. Cradle-snatching. The words still had the power to hurt, even over the distance of the intervening years. But then they had devastated her, leaving her raw and humiliated, aching with a frustration she barely understood, and vowing never, ever to speak to him again.

But she had been hooked on Gabriel's own potent brand of dark sexuality, and like a true addict she hadn't been able to give up the source of her need. It hadn't mattered how many times the voice of reason told her she would be far happier if she found someone else, someone her own age, whose uncomplicated company she could enjoy as a distraction from this obsession that was eating into her soul, she just hadn't listened.

There had been no shortage of candidates for the role of Gabriel's replacement. Since she had started at art college she had been snowed under with invitations to clubs or films, a drink or a meal. But none of them had appealed. There had been no one else who had his blazing charisma, his lethally attractive looks, his mesmeric sexuality, and by the time her nineteenth birthday had come around she had known she couldn't hide her feelings any longer.

Her birthday.

Rachel's heart kicked sharply as she flicked on the light, illuminating the room she now used as her studio. It had looked so very different then.

No! She clamped down hard on the images that were already starting to rise to the surface of her mind. She didn't want to remember; didn't want to think about that night.

But she had to.

'Think about it, you fool!' she told herself fiercely. '*Think about it*! Remember how it was. Remember it all. Perhaps then you'll cure yourself once and for all of this sickness in the blood where Gabriel Tiernan is concerned!'

And in spite of her struggle to push them away, she knew she couldn't suppress her memories any longer. They were already breaking through into the full light of day, forcing her to look them squarely in the face...

CHAPTER FIVE

GABRIEL had been away for seven months. He was already planning on expanding the business in the States and had been working there ever since the start of the new year. But now he was back, and Rachel couldn't wait to see him.

She had taken full advantage of the opportunity afforded by his absence to give herself a complete makeover. She had dieted, exercised, restyled her hair, her make-up, invested in new clothes. Without vanity, she knew she looked good—the gauche, unsophisticated Rachel he had last seen left far, far behind.

The look on Gabriel's face when he first met her eyes was a start, but it was as nothing to the plot that she had for the following night—the actual date of her nineteenth birthday. Greg and Lydia had planned a large party at the weekend, but a family celebration dinner was to be held for just the four of them.

Rachel wore a slim, elegant column of a dress in wine-red silk, her own newest designs at her throat and earlobes, her hair sleek and smooth, and she knew she looked stunning. During the meal, as the champagne and congratulations flowed, she sparkled more and more with every second. It was clear that Gabriel couldn't take his eyes off her, though his behaviour was kept strictly within the bounds of what was decorous, much to her frustration.

Except for one comment at the end of the evening.

As he kissed her goodnight his lips lingered just slightly longer than was strictly necessary, and when he spoke it was with his mouth so close to her ear that his soft murmur could not be heard by the others present.

'You've grown up, little Rachel. You've turned into a woman while I was away, and a very beautiful woman at that. I can see that I'm going to have to rethink my attitude towards you very strongly. Perhaps we could get together to discuss it some time?'

She needed no further encouragement.

It was everything she had ever dreamed of. No birthday present she had received could have given one quarter as much happiness or excitement, and she couldn't wait for the opportunity to take him up on that 'discussion' he had suggested.

Her opportunity came the following night. Greg and Lydia were out at the theatre, after which they planned on a late dinner, and she and Gabriel were alone in the house.

Collecting a couple of bottles of champagne from the stocks laid in for the party, she made her way up to the attic, excitement bubbling up inside her. She didn't pause to knock, but simply pushed the sitting-room door open and bounced into the room.

'Hi! Not interrupting anything, am I?'

'Nothing important.'

He had obviously not been reading the book that lay open in his lap. It had clearly fallen from his hands while his thoughts had been elsewhere. Rachel dared to allow herself the indulgence of thinking they had been with her.

'I thought we'd have our own private celebration.'

'And what are we celebrating?' he enquired, in a soft drawl that made her shiver just to hear it.

'Well, the fact that you're home for one. And my birthday, of course. Yours too—for last week. I brought us something to drink.' She brandished the champagne in the air. 'After all, Greg's bought so much of the stuff for Saturday that they won't miss a couple of bottles. So if you'll just do the honours...'

It was as he got to his feet, moving to take the champagne from her, that a strange new awareness of his height and strength, the masculine force in those powerful shoulders, the broad chest, suddenly hit her in a very disturbing way. The colour faded from her cheeks.

'What is it, Rachel? You look like you've seen a ghost.'

The softness of his voice was reassuring. For a moment it had seemed as if a picture had slipped out of focus, but now, as she blinked hard, it slid back into place. This was *Gabriel*. The man she had loved for years.

'I've just realised I've forgotten the glasses,' she declared, with a laugh of embarrassment.

'Not to worry.' He was busy with the champagne as he spoke, strong hands dealing efficiently with the top of the bottle. 'I have some in the cabinet over there.'

'Of course.' Her composure slipped again for a moment. 'I'd forgotten that this was your own private bachelor pad—the place where you entertain all your lady-friends.'

The thought of the sleekly elegant beauties who seemed to flock round him clouded her eyes, turning them from silver to a smoky haze.

'Not *all* my lady-friends,' Gabriel corrected. 'Only a select few. A glass—quick!'

In the dash to catch the sparkling rush of champagne before it spilled over the top of the bottle Rachel felt some of her uncertainty evaporate. By the time she had a full glass in her hand she had found the nerve to ask the question that was uppermost in her mind.

'And am I included in that select group?'

'What do you think?'

His attention was on the second glass he was filling. Rachel took a large sip of the sparkling liquid, wrinkling her nose as the bubbles tickled it.

'Well, you used to let me up here whenever I wanted—to borrow books and stuff for college. But just lately…'

Her carefully rose-painted mouth made a petulant moue of protest.

'I seem to have been decidedly out of favour.'

'I've been away, Rachel,' Gabriel pointed out, indicating with a wave of his hand that she should take the chair opposite his. 'As you know very well. And when I've been here I've been hellishly busy dealing with things that have had to be neglected while I concentrate on my plans for America. And besides…'

The dark eyes lifted suddenly, locking with hers over the rim of her glass, freezing her movement, closing her throat so that she found she couldn't swallow.

'Things are no longer quite as simple as they used to be.' His voice had altered perceptibly, becoming an octave deeper, taking on a rough, husky edge.

'Why is that?' Rachel's question was accompanied by an arch, teasing smile.

'I'm sure you can guess.'

She was pretty sure that she could, but she didn't want to tempt fate by rushing in too soon. It would be so humiliating if she had misread all the signs, got everything totally wrong. So instead she opted for diversionary tactics for a while.

'Tell me, exactly what are you doing in America?' she asked, kicking off her shoes and curling her feet up under her in the dark green velvet-covered armchair. 'Setting up a branch of Tiernan's over there?'

'Branches—and shops with a difference. In fact I want them to be so different that Dad's totally opposed to the way I intend things to go.'

'Really?' She was genuinely intrigued now.

For some time she had been aware of the fact that the tension that was the result of Gabriel's hostility towards her mother seemed to have eased, but now a new and very different discord had grown up between him and his father. Now she saw that this had its roots in work matters.

'What are you doing that's so appalling?'

Gabriel's smile was wry, slightly lopsided, giving his hard-boned face a surprisingly boyish appeal.

'I've been trying to drag the company kicking and screaming into the twentieth century and to make it much less elitist.'

'It sounds exciting. What exactly are your plans?'

'I want to produce a more accessible set of designs. They'd have the same standard of production, of finish, but use much less expensive materials. It would be a range that would have all the elements of quality and style that Tiernan's have become famous for, but available at a much more affordable price.'

'Like the diffusion labels the couturiers produce?'

'Exactly.'

Her comment earned her a swift, flashing grin of approval that made her heart turn somersaults inside her chest.

'Not only would it give us another string to our bow, but it would provide an outlet for some very different, far more adventurous designs. We could afford to let them be influenced by street fashion, which would give the new pieces a sharper edge than the traditional stuff my father is so keen on.'

'And he's letting you do this?'

Gabriel's mouth twisted wryly.

'Not so much "letting" as giving me enough rope and hoping I'll hang myself. I have a large amount of my own money invested in this venture. If it fails I lose—heavily. But, equally, if it succeeds it'll be something Dad can't touch—it won't even have the Tiernan's name. The new stores are simply called T2.'

'It sounds just the sort of thing I'd like.' Rachel held out her glass to be refilled, her face alight, eyes glowing. 'I'd love to be involved in something like that.'

'Well, keep on with your studies and you could well end up doing just that. I'd certainly give you a job. You have real talent, Rachel, the sort that could take you right to the top.'

The praise was unexpected, sending a rush of hot colour to her cheeks, flooding her whole body with a sense of intoxication that had nothing to do with the champagne.

'You're flattering me.'

'No flattery,' he assured her. 'I only ever tell the exact truth—never exaggerate. You know you're talented, just as you know that you're beautiful. And you must know that that's a lethal combination, one that's hard to resist.'

This was even worse. Hastily Rachel raised her glass to her lips again, needing something to cool the betraying heat in her face. To her consternation she found it was empty.

'Can I have some more champagne, please?'

'Don't you think you've had enough?'

That question smacked too much of an almost parental attitude, making her purse her lips sulkily.

'I'm not a child any more, Gabriel. I'm nineteen.'

And to prove the point she got up and filled her own glass, not giving a damn whether he approved or not.

'I'm a woman—a fact that you don't seem to have grasped.'

'On the contrary. It's something of which I am only too well aware. The question is, what are we going to do about it?'

'Do?'

Confused grey eyes met intent brown ones so sharply that she could almost see the sparks in the air caused by the jarring clash.

'Tell me something, Rachel...'

Gabriel put his glass down on a nearby bookshelf and leaned back in his chair, his dark head resting on a cushion as he looked up at her.

'Would I be wrong in assuming that your presence here tonight isn't just a casual visit, but part of a deliberate campaign to make me aware of just how much of a woman you are?'

Dazed by the sharpness of his perception, Rachel

could only nod silently, gulping down another unwary mouthful of her drink.

'Every one of your actions, your smile, your eyes, every gesture, even the way you're dressed...'

The burning gaze slid down over the rich blue sleeveless dress she wore, over the deep V-neck, the buttons all the way down the front, then swung sharply back up to her burning face.

'They're all the sort of signals a woman uses to communicate the fact that she wants—expects—a particular sort of response from a man. And as there is no other male present I can only assume that *I* am the one you're signalling to.'

With a sense of shock Rachel realised that suddenly everything had changed. His relaxed, indolent quality had vanished. Instead, every inch of Gabriel's lean, powerful length was taut with a new sense of alertness, a forceful, dangerous air of expectancy that dried her mouth, made her heart seem to be beating high up in her throat.

'Is that it, Rachel? Do you want me to respond to you as a man does to a woman?'

Again she nodded silently, the power of speech having completely deserted her.

'Then why don't we dispense with the pussyfooting around?' His voice had sunk to a softly intent whisper. 'Drop the pretence that we don't know exactly why you're here...'

'Pretence?' The need to protest brought her ability to speak back in a rush. 'I'm not *pretending*!'

'No? Then prove it. Come here, Rachel,' he ordered when she hesitated, still unsure. 'Come here and kiss me.'

She had thought she would need no urging, but suddenly, now, with her dream so close to coming true at last, her nerve deserted her. The small space between them suddenly seemed like a gaping chasm, too huge, too dangerous to be crossed on legs that weren't quite strong enough to support her.

Dark-chocolate eyes watched her all the time, making her pulse leap, race frantically, so that her blood pounded inside her head like waves beating against a rocky shore.

Licking dry lips, she stood above him, looking down into those deep, impenetrable eyes. Then slowly, nervously, inch by cautious inch, she lowered her head and brushed his mouth gently with hers.

Immediately the tingle of excitement ran along the line of every nerve, her heart lurching in pure delight. But Gabriel, it seemed, was not so easily satisfied. There was no softening of those firm lips under hers. His only response was a growl of displeasure deep in his throat.

'For God's sake, Rachel!' he muttered harshly. 'You kiss like a child! If you want to prove that you're a woman then bloody well kiss like one. If not—'

But he never finished the sentence. Rachel silenced him in the only way she could think of—by bringing her mouth down on his, but more forcefully this time, crushing his words before they were spoken.

This time, as she kissed him, she sent her thoughts back to that kiss under the mistletoe in order to remember what it had felt like, how she knew he wanted it to be. She would hide her fear, her lack of knowledge under the pretence...

But the pretence lasted barely the length of a couple of seconds. Within the space of a heartbeat or two, that rush of delight had conquered her fear, driving before it all uncertainty or hesitation.

The crackling flame that licked along her body tracked through every nerve, every cell, heating them to the white-hot intensity of molten gold before she had time to draw another breath. Her hands reached for Gabriel, tangling in the dark hair, pulling his face closer to hers as her tongue sought the sleek warmth of his yielding mouth.

'Better?' she demanded breathlessly, when the need to breathe forced them apart—she had no idea how much later.

'Better,' he agreed on a shaken laugh. 'But I believe we can still improve on things.'

And, reaching up, he caught hold of her, pulling her down onto his lap and settling her against him so that he could kiss her again, more thoroughly this time.

If she had thought that his Christmas kiss had been exciting, then it faded into insignificance when compared with this concentrated assault on her senses. One moment Gabriel's lips were soft and enticing, charming a response from her, and the next they were hard and fierce, bruising her softness with their force, demanding a passion to match his own.

Then again they changed, this time to a richly erotic sensitivity, one that seemed to drain her very soul from her body, flooding her mind with heat so that she was incapable of thought.

And all the time his hands caressed and smoothed over her body, burning wild, heated trails over her exposed skin, burning through the linen of her dress when they paused to cup the softness of her breasts. One long finger traced the outline of the V-neck, slid into the space between her buttons, making her catch her breath at the feel of his touch on her sensitised flesh.

Her skirt had rucked up beneath her, exposing her legs, completely bare of tights because of the warmth of the day. Beneath her she could feel the soft corduroy of Gabriel's trousers, and beneath that the hardness of the heated swelling that pressed against her thigh in eloquent testimony, if she needed it, of the effect she was having on him.

A shudder that combined both desire and apprehension shook her slim body. This was no hasty, exploratory fumble between two inexperienced adolescents. She could be in no doubt that her partner was all male, with a grown man's needs.

It was a hunger she must decide whether to match, step by step, or get away from—*now*.

Almost as if he had read her thoughts, in that same moment she heard Gabriel draw in a deep, uneven breath as he lifted his mouth from hers and stared deep into her smokily clouded eyes.

'Decision time,' he said, in a voice that was distinctly ragged round the edges. 'I need to know now, while I can still behave like a gentleman, if that's what you want.'

Rachel's whole being went very still; her eyes locked with his. But on the white skin of one exposed thigh a softly delicate fingertip moved in a slow, heated circle, round and round, over and over again. And it was on that one tiny point that all her thoughts, all her feelings were centred as he spoke again.

'You have to make your mind up, Rachel—girl or woman; it's up to you. But be very sure which one you choose, because once you've decided you're committed—and there's no going back.'

CHAPTER SIX

NO GOING back.

The words hung in the air, heavy with significance. No matter which way she turned, she couldn't escape them, and she knew that the answer she gave would change her future for ever.

'Well, Rachel, what is it to be?'

It was soft-voiced, apparently calm. Even his hands had stopped moving and now lay completely still on the arms of the chair. He was putting no pressure on her, either physical or mental. It was her choice and hers alone.

In the silence of the darkening room the steady ticking of a clock seemed unnaturally loud. Its rhythmical marking of time matched and echoed the powerful, regular beat of Gabriel's heart underneath her fingertips where they lay on the soft black cotton of his T-shirt.

No going back.

In the end, it was something as simple as the loss of that tiny caress on her leg that decided her. Without it her skin felt so cold, totally bereft.

The aching sense of emptiness that began at this focal point radiated along the path of every nerve in her body, racing inwards to the deepest, most intimate heart of her femininity and setting up a hungry yearning that just one thing could appease.

'Yes,' she said softly, so softly that at first he didn't catch her response and frowned his uncertainty.

'*Yes...*' she began again, more firmly this time.

Already some change in her expression, in her body, must have alerted him. He didn't wait for her to finish, but pulled her against him once more. This time he captured her mouth with a wild ferocity that might have combined with any doubts to create a flaring panic that would have had her fighting for her freedom, her safety.

But Rachel had no such doubts. On the contrary, she welcomed the wildness of his kiss, drew from it a courage that fed her own inner hunger. Dark currents, unguessed at until now, flooded through her veins, awakening needs she had only dreamed of, arousing a deep, burning hunger that was so sharp it was touched with pain.

'Are you sure this is what you want?' Gabriel's voice was huskily raw against her skin.

When she could only nod numbly, her ability to speak exhausted, he levered himself to his feet, taking her with him so that she leaned against the strength of his body for support.

The next moment she found herself swung up into his arms and carried into the next room, Gabriel shouldering the door open with an impatient gesture before he lowered her slowly onto his bed.

'Woman it is, then,' he muttered, pulling the black T-shirt up and over his head in one fluid movement. 'There are only so many times a man can say no to temptation.'

As he joined her on the green and gold duvet cover Rachel's heart was beating such a crazy tattoo that it obliterated thought, leaving her incapable of anything beyond feeling. After so many long months of dreaming, the reality was almost more than she could bear. He was actually here, beside her, hers to kiss, to hold, to touch...

The feel of the heated velvet of his skin against her fingertips was devastating, mixing with the after effects of the champagne to create the most potent, mind-blowing force she had ever experienced. She wanted to touch him everywhere, to caress every inch of him, to feel the hard, starkly aroused body against her own.

'Rachel...' A shaken whisper sounded in her ear. 'Take it steady...'

But she didn't want to take *anything* steady. And her whirling mind rejected that softly voiced caution. She was no longer the child he had once thought her; she was all woman, female through and through. She gloried in the wonder of it, the delight, the strength.

Her breasts seemed heavy and tight, the hard nipples stinging with the need for his touch, the warmth of his mouth. When the cool brush of the evening air against her skin brought home to her that the linen dress had been discarded, and with it the brief scraps of lace that were all she had worn beneath it, she cried her delight out loud, moving closer, slender limbs tangling with his stronger, hair-roughened ones.

She had never known such excitement, never experienced such uncontrolled yearning. Her body's greedy response to his stunned and bewildered her.

Where had she learned to react like this? To trail her fingers over the line of hard muscle and sinew and feel it jerk, watch it bunch under the path of her caress? What instinct had taught her exactly where and how to kiss in order to create the most effect, to draw from him the choking cry that revealed how close he was to losing control, the groan that indicated his total surrender?

She no longer even knew herself. Only the person she had become.

'Rachel...'

Her name seemed to be torn from Gabriel, an edge of desperation to his voice as her untutored hands moved lower, needing to know the full truth of him. She wanted to feel that alien, most masculine part of him both hard and soft against her tentative palm.

'Rachel!' This time it was a cry of warning, of protest. 'No. Touch me like that again and I...'

But it was a protest she didn't want to hear. Deliberately she increased the pressure of her caress, responding to some intuitive, primitive rhythm. Her hips moved under his, lifting to press upwards against the heat and strength of his arousal.

Above her, his face was suddenly that of a stranger. All gentleness, all patience was stripped away, leaving behind nothing but stark desire, blazing passion.

'Oh, God! Angel, I warned you—!'

The pain of his frantic possession of her seemed to rip her soul from her body. It took with it all the golden heat, the soaring excitement, and left her cold, desolate and shocked, the force of her disappointment like a bruising blow to her heart.

How could this have happened? How could something she had wanted so badly, that had promised so much, turn so sour? How could she be left here, lost, abandoned and betrayed, while he went on alone to the fulfilment that had seemed just on the horizon and yet now was totally out of reach?

Furious, hurt and outraged, she clenched her hands into tight fists, pounding them violently against the broad, naked shoulders that still pinned her to the bed.

'I hate you! I hate you! *This* isn't what I wanted...'

'I know...'

It was a deep, harsh sigh, one that seemed to have been wrenched out of him as he rolled to one side so that she was free to move.

'Believe me, I know.'

And before she could escape his arms closed round her and she felt herself gathered close, crushed up against the naked wall of his chest and held so tightly she could hardly breathe. The strength of his muscles held her even when she tightened her own against him, and she had no option but to lie still.

Later, when his harsh breathing had evened out, when the frantic racing of his heart had slowed, he shifted his position carefully, taking her face in both his hands and cupping it gently as he drew it towards his.

'I'm sorry, sweetheart,' he murmured, pressing soft, impossibly tender kisses over her tear-stained face. 'So very sorry. I wouldn't have had that happen for the world. But you were so beautiful, so innocently sensual.

You opened to me so sweetly, so generously that I lost my head. I was greedy—too selfish. But I promise you that next time it will be so very different.'

'No!'

There would be no next time. She couldn't go through that ever again. Frantically she shook her head from side to side, her bright hair splaying out against the pillow. '*No*!'

But unbelievably, impossibly, those kisses were already working on her resistance. They bewitched and enticed, hypnotising, cajoling, drawing from her the fragile beginnings of a response that she had thought was gone for good, never to be revived.

'Hush, darling,' Gabriel soothed. 'Trust me. Let me show you what it should be like. Let me show you how it feels when there is no pain, only pleasure. Let me give you the delight, the wonder you gave me. Please trust me. I promise I won't let you down.'

And when he punctuated his words with kisses that tugged at her soul, when his hands were already moving over her sensitised body, touching, stroking, smoothing, she knew she couldn't find the strength or even the desire to protest. She could only respond, feeling her senses flower under his caress, opening to him like a delicate bud to the sun. The gentle heat that flooded her drove away the icy sense of loss of moments earlier.

Before she had quite realised what was happening, she was writhing sensually under his touch, tiny murmurs of surprised pleasure escaping her. Murmurs that turned into sighs and moans, finally, unbelievably, building to cries of delight. Delight that was mixed with a hunger that licked through her body like a flame—growing, demanding…

Dimly she was aware of hot kisses trailing over her skin, up the curve of one breast to close over the tight nub at its tip. She couldn't control her response, convulsing in helpless reaction to the sharp, sweet agony of desire that speared through her.

Taking advantage of her total loss of inhibition, her lack of any fear or apprehension, Gabriel slid the silken heat of his body into hers in one strong movement that left her gasping. But this time her response was not one of pain, but of disbelief and wonderment at the perfect sense of completion.

'That's better!' His voice was shaking, dark laughter and even darker triumph underlining the words. 'Much better. But there's one more thing...'

'More!' Rachel murmured the word in sheer disbelief. *More*? How could there be any more sensation, any more pleasure? She didn't believe it was possible.

But Gabriel showed her that it was.

Where before he had been all passion and *im*patience, so now he was pure patience, pure generosity. He made every move slow and deliberate, carefully designed to heighten the feelings she was experiencing, add to her delight.

His mouth kissed, nibbled, sucked, even snatched tiny, teasing bites at her skin. At the same time his hands smoothed, stroked, circled over every intimate pleasure spot she knew and some she'd had no idea existed.

She was lost, adrift on a glowing sea of pure eroticism. She could do nothing but let the waves of heat carry her closer and closer to some incandescent destination that she was just beginning to believe she might actually reach.

As if he read her need in her face, Gabriel tightened his body, his thrusts taking on a more potent, rhythmic intensity. His caresses grew harder, more urgent and the glowing point on the horizon came nearer, nearer—until, in the moment she touched it, there was nothing but a blazing spiral of sensation that convulsed her body, drawing her out of herself and throwing her into another dimension entirely.

The sharp, piercing ecstasy took her higher and higher until, at its peak, she actually felt that she might die. Either that or her mind must surely shatter, splintering into tiny crystalline pieces, each of which pulsed with that same brilliant light.

But somehow she remained whole, and slowly, slowly, she came back down to earth to find herself held securely in Gabriel's arms, her body still intimately joined to his. His breathing was as ragged as her own, his heart pounding in the same desperate, primitive rhythm of fulfilment.

'Now, that…' he said softly when he managed to speak, his voice still thickened by the passion they had shared. 'That was what you really came up here for, wasn't it?'

'Rachel? Are you all right?'

Coming from behind her, the soft-voiced question was so shockingly unexpected that it was like a blow to her head, jarring her brutally. With a sharp cry she whirled round to confront the dark, masculine figure who had come into the room unobserved while she had been absorbed in her thoughts.

'I'm sorry—I didn't mean to frighten you.'

Steadying hands closed over her arms, holding her upright when she might have fallen off balance.

'Is everything OK?'

It was the voice she had heard in her memories. But where before it had been raw with passion, then rich with dark velvet satisfaction, now it was cool and controlled, with just a thread of concern shading it.

'I…'

'You took so long finding those designs I was worried. I thought perhaps you might be unwell, that the strain of today—'

'I'm fine!'

Rachel shook her head violently to drive away the clinging remnants of her memories. Pulling herself from Gabriel's hold, she glared at him, grey eyes blazing like diamonds.

'I'm absolutely fine.' She could wish for a little less

shrillness to prove the point. 'And you have no right to be up here...'

His frown was darkly ominous, sending a shiver down her spine.

'And why is that?' he asked harshly. 'My father died less than a week ago; we only buried him this morning. Already there are restrictions on where I can go in this house that was once my home! *This* was my room.'

'I know...'

Guilt twisted painfully inside her, her conscience reproving her sharply. But all the same she knew she didn't want him here. Here where the echoes of the past still seemed to linger, where she could almost believe she could see the images of their long-ago selves hovering, spectre-like, between their present day forms.

'But it's *mine* now.'

The glare he turned on her was wild and ferocious as forked lightning, making her feel that it might actually have the power to shrivel her into a heap of ashes on the floor.

'And that's the problem, isn't it, sweet Rachel?' His cynicism slashed at her. 'Now that you and your mama have taken possession of the house—'

'No! Oh, no!' She couldn't bear him to believe that. 'Oh, Gabriel, please—you mustn't think that! This is your home, more than it ever was mine, and it always will be!'

'We both know that's not true...'

But something had distracted him. Those dark eyes that had been fixed on her face now slid away to take in his surroundings for the first time, narrowing swiftly as he became fully aware of the room.

'You certainly redecorated thoroughly.'

Rachel winced at the undertone that turned the conventional comment into something else entirely. She knew what he was seeing, but couldn't begin to guess at what interpretation he might put on it.

When it had first been suggested that she take over

the attic apartment, she had rejected the idea out of hand. The memories the rooms evoked for her were too powerful, too painful, for her ever to be able to settle there, let alone sleep in the place that had once been Gabriel's 'bachelor pad'.

But Greg had been determined. He had kept on and on about the idea, refusing to take no for an answer. Eventually, over a period of more than a year, he had finally worn down her objections and he'd arranged to have it redecorated for her twenty-first birthday present. However, there had been one fundamental change she had insisted on. A change that had at least gone part way towards eradicating the lingering ghosts she dreaded.

'What made you decide to change the rooms around?'

'This one gets more light.'

A nervous gesture indicated the huge window, taking up almost all of one wall, that had been put in since he had last been there.

'I need it for when I'm working on my designs.'

It was a perfectly justifiable explanation. And why shouldn't it be, when it contained a large part of the truth? But it wasn't all of it, and it was the thought of what she was holding back that had her shifting uncomfortably from one foot to another on the polished wood of her studio floor.

'It's very effective.'

If Gabriel guessed at the real reasoning behind her decision, nothing of his thoughts showed in his voice. It was as bland and casual as if she were a stranger he had just met, someone whose house he was seeing for the very first time.

'I—like to think so.'

The way the sentence broke up in the middle gave too much away, bringing those deep-set eyes back to her face in a swiftly assessing stare.

'Calm down, Rachel,' he said, obviously misinterpreting the reason for her nervousness. 'I told you—I won't pounce.'

'I know you won't!' she flared. 'You won't because I have no intention of ever letting you near me! There's nothing to be gained by it. It's over—dead and gone. And that's why I want you out. Out of my room and out of my life.'

She didn't know quite what she'd expected his reaction to be. If it had ever crossed her mind that he might actually do as she said, and leave, then she'd dismissed the foolish thought as swiftly as it had arisen. What she hadn't planned for was the cynical way his mouth curled, the dark scrutiny he turned on her face.

'If I could believe that then I'd feel a lot better about things.'

'Believe it!' she flung at him, desperate to hide the sudden flare of panic she was prey to.

She didn't know what was troubling her more: the fact that he still didn't believe she no longer had any feelings for him or the thought that the lack of such emotions was what he wanted most.

'Believe that there's nothing—*nothing* in my heart for you any more.'

The change in his face was shocking, terribly disturbing. Even though she knew it was deliberately calculated to have just that effect it still tore at her heart, as if the shadows in his eyes had been real and not coldly assumed.

'Oh, Rachel...' he began very softly.

But she'd had enough. Past and present swirled together in one fateful combination.

'*No*! I don't want to listen! I don't want to hear a word you've got to say. I just want you to go...'

With the flat of her palms against the wall of his chest, she pushed at him hard, desperation giving her strength.

'Go on! Get out—*out*!'

Because her sudden force had taken him by surprise, he actually took a step backwards towards the door. Just one. But then he stopped dead, resisting her attack with an insulting lack of effort as he reached out to capture her wrists in a grip of steel.

'Rachel, stop it!'

She didn't have any choice. She couldn't have resisted him if she'd tried; her attempts to escape were useless against his easy strength. And so she gave in, subsiding into mutinous silence, her jaw still stubbornly set.

Dark brown eyes blazed down into crystalline grey ones, and there was a long, frozen moment during which Rachel could only stare up at Gabriel in shocked confusion. Her hands still rested on the fine linen of his shirt and she could feel the heat of his body, the faint roughness of his body hair underneath her fingertips.

How many times had she heard of a shiver of awareness, a frisson feathering down the spine of someone because of some sudden, close contact? This was nothing like that. It was nowhere near as gentle, as delicate.

On the contrary, it felt like a fierce, harsh sensation, a rough scraping over her sensitive nerves as if some metallic hand, a brutal claw, had scoured her skin from her bones.

She had never been more aware in her life. So much so that now she saw her room so clearly it was as if a spotlight had suddenly been switched on.

She saw the desk by the window, the flowers on the cupboard, the bright paintings on the walls. Through the window was the expanse of the garden, at the far end of which, behind the trees, flowed the wide river Thames.

But clearest and sharpest of all she saw Gabriel standing before her, the white shirt tugged loose at the neck to expose the strong, tanned lines of his throat, the soft fall of his dark hair onto the face she had once loved so deeply. The light from the window seemed to have thrown his features into such sharp relief that it hurt to look at them.

'Gabriel...'

But the words wouldn't come. Because that was when

she knew once and for all that she had lied both to him and to herself. Nothing had died, nor was it ever likely to. It was all still there, barely hidden, so that all she had to do was just scratch at the surface and it would bubble up again, exposed once more.

She might have forced her feelings to the bottom of her mind four and a half years before. And since then she had let layer after protective layer of routine, daily life, build up on top of them in order to conceal them from her, but they had never disintegrated, never gone away. Instead they had stayed buried like some hibernating creature, huddled away, just waiting.

Until now, when just the sight of Gabriel, the sound of his voice had acted like a catalyst, breaking into their hiding place and driving them to claw their way to the surface, back into life all over again.

'Oh, Gabriel,' she sighed, staring down at her hands still on his chest. 'Why did you ever have to come back?'

'Believe me, if I could have stayed away, I would.'

One surprisingly gentle hand slid under her chin, lifting her face towards his, but she closed her eyes swiftly, fearful that he would see the tears swimming in them.

'Rachel, I don't want to hurt you.'

'You don't want...' Bitter laughter caught in her aching throat. 'Have you ever thought of what you've done already?'

The silence that followed her accusation went on for so long that she had to look up—into a face that seemed suddenly bleached of all colour.

'Oh, God, Rachel, no. Don't say that. Don't—'

He stopped dead as one weak tear seeped from the corner of her eye, and she saw his strangely clouded gaze follow its slow slide down her cheek. He swallowed hard just once.

'Rachel...'

Her name became a deep groan as he bent his dark head to kiss away the tiny diamond of moisture that lay beside her mouth. His lips were soft and warm and infinitely gentle, and in spite of herself she couldn't control her impulse to turn her face towards him. The movement made his caress slide over her skin until their mouths met.

'Rachel!'

It was a very different sound. One that seemed shaken and strangely hesitant, disturbingly vulnerable. Even as she formed the thought she wanted to shake her head to drive it away. It was impossible! Gabriel hesitant? Rarely. Vulnerable? Never!

But she couldn't make the movement. Instead she found her face captured, held softly prisoner between two warm, strong hands. Long fingers slipped into her hair, hard palms curved against her cheeks. And his mouth was on hers again, gentle as before, touching it softly, delicately, as if tasting the finest wine, a taste he wanted to linger over, to savour.

And it was not enough. It could never be enough. Having once known the full brilliance of the blazing passion this man could ignite in her, how could she ever be satisfied with something that had only the soft light of a flickering candle?

With a small, choking cry she caught her arms up around his neck, fingers lacing in the dark silk of his hair. Exerting all her strength, she pulled his face down to hers, forcing him to increase the pressure of his mouth.

Instantly it was as if a wild electrical storm had broken directly overhead. As if she was bathed in lightning from her head to her toes.

Gabriel's kiss could no longer be described as anything remotely resembling hesitant. There was nothing vulnerable about the way his lips took hers. Instead they were greedy, seeking, *demanding* the response she gave so willingly. Her mouth opened under his, yielding to the intimate caress she craved every bit as much as he did.

At such a white-hot intensity, it was inevitable that very soon simple kissing would not be enough. Rachel's breasts felt swollen where they were crushed against his chest, and they ached with the same hunger that pulsed throughout her lower body. She couldn't bear to leave even so much as an inch to separate her from Gabriel, and crushed herself hard up against him, hearing his breath escape in a deep, ragged sigh.

The heat of his palms was on her neck, her shoulders, burning into the soft flesh of her arms exposed by the short sleeves of her dress. His hands slid over her back, moulding her even closer to him before moving downwards, hard fingers digging into the curves of her hips, her buttocks.

There was no mistaking the hard evidence of the desire he felt, and as she moaned her delight his mouth slid away from hers, trailing lower, lower…

'Gabriel…'

'Oh, God in heaven, no!'

Her shaken voice clashed with his violent curse, the sound shattering the heated silence of the room.

A moment later he had wrenched his head up, pulling away from her with a ferocity that tore agonisingly at every nerve.

'Gabriel…?'

Still not quite registering what had happened, she reached for him again, but once more he caught her hands, enclosing her wrists in a brutal grip as he held them well away from him.

'I said *no*!'

He dragged in another raw, harsh-edged breath and swallowed it down hard. The ebony darkness of his eyes had deepened to the black of onyx, glittering with a wild, febrile light that chilled the blood in her veins.

'This has to stop right now.'

'Stop?'

Not like this! Not for a second time. It was as if she

had gone back over four years in time, back to that dreadful moment here, in the very same place.

She had taken months, years to recover from that. In fact she was just beginning to realise that she hadn't really recovered at all. She couldn't go through it again. This new rejection was more than she could bear.

'Why? Why must it stop?'

'Because I don't—'

'You don't?' she cut in, her voice sliding up a scale. '*You* don't! Always you, and what you want. What about—'

'Rachel...'

'No!'

Misery giving her a strength she hadn't known she possessed, she twisted free, the force of her action sending her halfway across the room.

'Don't you "Rachel" me! I won't listen to you ever again—because you *lied*!'

The pain burned like acid in her heart so that she didn't care what she said, needing only to express the agony, heedless of the possible consequences of her outburst.

'You lied when you said that you didn't want me—that you didn't fancy me at all.'

'Did I ever say that?'

His calmness brought her up short. Somehow he seemed to have regained his composure in an unbelievably short space of time. Once more that cold, hard mask had slid down over his features, transforming them into the marble face of a Greek statue, disturbingly blank and unrevealing.

'Or is that just what you thought you heard? How you interpreted what I said?'

His tone made her wince, the freezing precision with which the words were formed falling like the cruel lash of ice against her delicate skin.

'Well, if I ever *did* give you the idea that I didn't want you then, yes, I *was* lying—through my teeth. I ''fancy'' you, as you so crudely put it, like hell. So much that it hurts not to have you. But I'll never—*never*—do anything about it. You're dangerous, Rachel, just too bloody dangerous.'

'Dangerous?' Rachel couldn't believe what she was hearing. 'Me? But how could I ever...?'

'It's who you are and what you bring with you that causes the problems, angel. You come trailing chains of risk, complications that could tangle up my life and drag me down to a living hell. I've been there once before and I never want to go through it again. So when I say this has to stop, I mean it is the *end*—right now!'

'But, Gabriel...'

She couldn't help herself; she had to reach out, to try to clasp his hand so as to plead with him. But he guessed at her movement and reacted swiftly, so that her fingers only managed to close over his arm.

'But nothing!'

His tone told her all she needed to know, even without the added bitter emphasis in the way that he shook off her restraining hand with a cold cruelty that stabbed at her heart.

'*It stops here*, Rachel. Once and for all. I never want to touch you again!'

CHAPTER SEVEN

How could she have let it happen again?

The question haunted Rachel through the long dark hours of the night. Through the sleepless time spent recalling Gabriel's appearance in her room, his kiss and her own uncontrolled response to it.

Would she never learn from the past, from all that had happened before? Surely that should have taught her once and for all that Gabriel Tiernan was not to be trusted. He was a man who used women for his own pleasure, picking them up and then discarding them at will, without a care for their feelings. And she had let him do that to her *twice*.

And this time she didn't even have the defence of naivety to hide behind. She was no longer a foolish adolescent in the throes of her first awareness of passion. Then, obsessed with the object of her fantasies, she had been incapable of thinking beyond him, of seeing anything else that went on around her.

They had almost been caught out that first time. In the early hours of the morning Gabriel had heard Greg's car pull up outside and had woken her up hurriedly. After a hasty scramble for her clothes, she had almost tumbled down the stairs in her haste to gain the safety of her own room where she had lain, hugging her excitement to herself, until she had fallen asleep and dreamed of the wonderful future that lay ahead of her.

The change had come within twenty-four hours.

She had woken as full of bubble and fizz as the champagne they had shared, and had bounced through the day with a blithe smile on her face, throwing herself into the preparations for her party with a bright enthusiasm. The only fly in the ointment had been the fact that Gabriel was conspicuous by his absence, though that had been easily explained by the fact that both he and his father were extremely busy at work.

But when he had appeared, at dinner that night, he'd been cool and surprisingly distant, barely glancing in her direction and only addressing a few, brief comments towards her. His behaviour had been light years away from the ardent lover of the night before.

Distinctly peeved, Rachel had waylaid him in the hall when they'd moved from the dining room to the lounge for coffee.

'Gabriel, what's going on? What's wrong?'

'Wrong?' His tone was as cool as his smile. 'Don't be silly, Rachel. Nothing's *wrong*. But we will have to be rather circumspect in front of your mother for a while. You know she and I have never seen eye to eye over anything, so it's going to take her some time to come round to the idea of the two of us together.'

Obliged to see the sense in what he had said, she had no choice but to accept, unwillingly, the wisdom of the path he counselled. But the next day things went from bad to worse.

She arrived home from college to an atmosphere that was positively rank with tension. Her mother and Greg had obviously had a major row, and although by dinner-time they were at least speaking, it was with a stiff politeness that made her feel distinctly uncomfortable.

Gabriel had clearly thought better of even joining them for the awkward meal. He drove off into the night without any explanation of where he was going, and he didn't return until the early hours of the following morning. How late he was, Rachel had no idea. She had tried to stay awake until he got back, but sleep had overcome her around two a.m., when he still wasn't home.

But the next day was the Saturday of her party, and all the rows in the world couldn't dampen her spirits as she dressed for the event.

The silver lace slip of a dress she had chosen was everything she had hoped it would be. It was shaped very simply, the shoestring straps revealing the creamy skin of her shoulders, the beautiful material skimming her breasts and hips, the short skirt showing off long, slim legs, lightly tanned like her arms by the warmth of the sun over the past couple of weeks.

With her hair falling in loose curls around her face and neck, and make-up used to subtly emphasise wide, luminous eyes, she knew she looked better than she had ever done in her life before. She fastened silver earrings of her own design at her lobes, slipped the matching delicate bracelet around her wrist, and smiled at herself in the mirror.

'No more little girl!' she told her reflection. She looked sophisticated, sensual and, most important, very, very grown-up.

She couldn't wait to show herself off to Gabriel. In spite of his resolve to be reticent, surely he would have to let slip something of what he felt when he saw her!

So she was stunned and bewildered when, as she twirled in front of her mother and Greg in the sitting room before anyone arrived, a cold, hard voice came from the open doorway, deflating all her excitement like air escaping from a pricked balloon.

'Don't you think it's rather tarty?'

It hurt. Hurt badly.

Stumbling to a halt, she turned reproachful grey eyes in his direction. There was playing it cool, but this was taking it too far!

'It's nothing of the sort!'

She was glad that she had started to speak as she was still turning. Because from the moment she actually set eyes on him all her ability to think deserted her in a rush. She could only stand and stare, completely transfixed.

She had never seen Gabriel in such formal evening wear before, and so wasn't prepared for the stunning effect of the tailored black and white when displayed on a tall, potently masculine frame. The dark brown hair had a new sheen and vibrancy when compared to the stark colouring, and his perfectly fitted suit enhanced the strong lines of his broad chest, narrow waist and long, long legs.

It was impossible not to think of the actuality of the powerful body underneath the elegant clothes, the erotic memory bringing a burning wash of heat up into Rachel's face. Swallowing hard, she tried again.

'I can wear what I like! I'm an adult now.'

An unfortunate remark, that. It came too close to things she had said—things they had both said—that night in his room. And from the way one dark brow lifted sardonically it was clear that Gabriel was thinking of exactly the same thing.

'You look like you're out on the pull!' he scorned. 'That "dress"...'

His harsh travesty of a laugh made it plain that he thought the description totally inaccurate.

'That slip of material is sexual provocation pure and simple. Lydia...'

To Rachel's astonishment he turned and appealed to her mother.

'Are you prepared to let your daughter appear in public dressed—or should I say undressed—like that?'

Lydia's smile was pure ice, her grey eyes distant.

'As Rachel says, she's nineteen now. She can choose her own clothes. Really, Gabriel, I think you're being rather old-fashioned. But then, I can't expect a man of your age to appreciate the sort of fashion that attracts young girls.'

And suddenly Rachel realised just what Gabriel was doing. He was playing devil's advocate, taking the opposite side to the one he really ascribed to, so that no one could ever suspect that she meant more to him than the schoolgirl he had so condescendingly tolerated.

Once she knew that, then his scorn, his apparent disapproval didn't hurt any more. And when Greg, too, took her part against his son she even turned a wide, defiant smile in his direction, laughing up into his darkly withdrawn face.

'You're outnumbered! The dress stays. But if you're *very* good then I'll let you have a dance with me to make up for your defeat!'

Once the party actually started she soon forgot about the minor spat that had preceded it. Caught up in the excitement, the hugs and kisses and cries of 'Happy Birthday', the seemingly endless stream of presents, she didn't have time to stop and wonder about Gabriel's attitude.

It was only much later that she recalled how his eyes had met hers so stonily, no gleam of amusement lightening their darkness, no trace of warmth softening his response to her. He couldn't really have *meant* what he'd said about her dress—could he?

Once the doubt had taken root in her mind, she began to notice other things as well.

There was the way he kept stiffly away from her, far more than was necessary to convince their parents that they were nothing but friends. The uncanny knack he had developed of never being around when a dance ended and she could move on to a new partner. That set, cold expression that never cracked into a smile. And the way he had of looking through her as if she simply didn't exist.

Well, she would show him! She didn't know what was bugging him, but she wouldn't care! It was her party and she was damn well going to enjoy it.

And so she set herself to indulging in a whirl of activity, dancing every dance with someone new, drinking champagne as if it were going out of style. She laughed outrageously at the slightest witticism, and flirted even more outrageously with anyone who showed the slightest interest.

It had no effect. Gabriel just leaned against the wall

at the far side of the ballroom and glowered, dark brows drawn together, ebony eyes deep and impenetrable. The only time he spoke to her was after she sashayed past him to refresh her drink, pausing only to glare at him in indignant reproach.

'Where have you been hiding all evening? Don't you think it's time you and I had a birthday dance together?'

'You seem to be doing all right for partners as it is.'

'Oh, yes, I'm having a wonderful time.' She hid the sharp sting of disappointment behind an air of bravado. 'Now, if you'll excuse me, I want some more wine.'

'Is that wise?' Gabriel growled reprovingly, directing a very pointed frown at her newly empty glass. 'Hadn't you better ease up? After all, you know champagne goes straight to your head.'

Spurred on by some dreadful imp of mischief, Rachel raised her glass in a pantomime of a toast, grey eyes translucent with wicked mockery.

'It goes straight to other, more interesting bits of me as well!' she declared, with a provocative wriggle of her hips.

That brought an even deeper, darker frown to the already hard lines of his face.

'I think we'd better talk, Rachel.'

'Talk? I've got better things to do. I'm having fun!'

'After the party—before you go to bed.'

It sounded too much like a command for her to accept willingly, and she arched a critical eyebrow.

'That's hardly the way to arrange a romantic assignation, dear! A lady likes a little more wooing…'

'Rachel…'

The ominous undertone warned her she was in danger of going too far, and she *did* want to spend some time alone with him if she possibly could.

'All right—after the party.'

But even as she spoke rebellion reasserted itself, and she couldn't resist needling him just one more time in revenge for his comment about her dress.

'That is, if I don't get a better offer,' she declared, and flounced away again before the thunderstorm that she could see brewing behind his eyes could finally break and devastate her once and for all.

But worse was to follow.

A short time later, when the band took a break and everyone went in to supper, Rachel suddenly realised that Gabriel was nowhere to be seen. A few cautious, carefully casual questions provided the information that he had last been seen talking to Amanda Bryant, the older sister of one of Rachel's college-friends.

'She was practically eating him up,' Becky reported, a salacious delight dripping from the words. 'I mean, he's such a hunk, and you know what Manda's like.'

She knew only too well, Rachel thought miserably. Becky's sister was a tall, sultry-looking brunette with a voluptuous figure that was being shown off to great advantage by a clinging black velvet sheath.

'Then they took off.' Becky waggled her eyebrows wildly to indicate just *why* she thought they had left in such a hurry. 'I know Manda was pretty bored. I heard her telling Gabriel that kids' parties really just weren't her thing.'

Kids' parties. If there had been a comment guaranteed to rub salt in Rachel's wounds, then that was it.

'Well, they're too old and stuffy for us,' she declared forcefully, trying desperately to save face. 'Practically middle-aged!'

But still she refused to believe that Gabriel's behaviour was anything more than a careful cover-up. After all, she told herself, what better way to convince a disapproving parent that there was nothing between them than by being seen very obviously dancing attendance on someone else?

It would have helped if she could convince herself, but it didn't work. What was left of the party was spoiled, and she was glad when the end of the evening finally arrived and everyone went home.

Gabriel still had not returned, but she seemed to be the only one concerned by his absence. She couldn't wait for him any longer. It was already well into the morning of a new day.

'I think I'll get straight off to bed, if you don't mind.'

She prayed that her mother and Greg would put her behaviour down to post-celebration lassitude, knowing she couldn't bear to stay and chat about how well things had gone.

'I'm absolutely worn out! Thank you both for a wonderful party.'

She *was* exhausted. But somehow sleep eluded her long after Greg and Lydia had gone to bed too. This time she was still awake when she heard Gabriel's key in the lock, his heavy footsteps on the stairs.

Briefly she tensed, wondering if he would come to her room. But the sound went on past the landing, up the second flight of stairs to the attic.

For long moments Rachel fought an internal war with herself. If she went up now, it would be just playing into his hands. He would probably laugh at her, tell her that she should have had more faith in him—worse, that she was being childish. She would do much better to wait and talk it all out calmly in the morning.

But she didn't feel calm, and she definitely didn't feel like waiting. Her whole body felt restless and unsettled, and thinking about Gabriel only made matters worse.

She had to see him now. Even if he laughed at her, it was better than lying here, feeling as if white-hot pins and needles were tormenting her. What she really needed was to be held in his arms and told how silly she'd been. After all, he had said he wanted to talk to her.

And then perhaps he would kiss her as he had done that night. Kiss her in a way that showed he thought her a real woman, no child at all. He would smooth his hands over her, ease the buttons on her nightdress from their fastenings...

The blood heating in her veins, she leapt out of bed.

Not troubling to pull on a robe, she crept silently out of her room, smiling faintly as she heard the echo of Greg's snores, audible even from the far end of the other corridor. In the space of a couple of uneven heartbeats she was up the stairs to the attic. But then, with her mission almost accomplished, she paused, momentarily losing her nerve.

That was when an unexpected sound came from behind the door. A cross between a choke and a squawk, hastily cut off before silence descended again.

'Gabriel?'

When there was no response, she wondered if perhaps she'd been mistaken—hearing things. Perhaps he hadn't come home at all and was still out somewhere. But then she heard the unmistakable sound of bedsprings adjusting to some movement, and, fired with sudden confidence, she swiftly turned the handle, pushing open the door.

'Gabriel?'

That strange noise again, but this time it was recognisable as a carefully muffled giggle, as if someone had their face buried in a pillow.

'Gabriel—are you there?'

'What is it, Rachel?'

Harsh and cynical, the voice came suddenly out of the darkness, making her jump like a fearful cat. The cold and unwelcoming edge to it sent a shiver over her skin, in spite of the warmth of the August night.

'I—just wanted to see you.'

'See me…?' It had an undertone that spoke of danger and threats, unforeseen horrors hidden at the bottom of a deep, dark sea. 'What the hell…?'

'Gabriel, please! I just want to—'

The words were smothered on her lips in the moment that Gabriel's shadowy figure moved on the bed. He reached out a hand and with an abrupt snap switched on the lamp that stood on the bedside table.

Blinking in the sudden brightness, Rachel couldn't believe what she saw. It couldn't be...

But then her blurred vision cleared and she focused, despairingly, disbelievingly, on the sight before her.

Gabriel was sitting up in bed, his broad chest bare, his dark hair falling in dishevelled disarray over his forehead. And at his side, just lifting her tousled head from the pillow, her olive skin flushed, her full mouth swollen with the evidence of fiercely passionate kisses, her long black hair tumbling around her shamelessly naked shoulders and breasts, was Amanda Bryant.

Gabriel!

She tried to say his name but shock had closed her throat, and though she opened her mouth no sound would come out.

Gabriel sighed his impatience.

'What is it, brat?' he drawled with hateful mockery. 'Couldn't you sleep? Well, if you wanted me to read you a bedtime story, then I'm sorry—no can do. As you can see, I'm busy right now...'

Turning to the woman at his side, he deliberately ran one long finger over the tops of her full breasts, smiling darkly as she writhed in sensual delight.

'I've things to do—adult things. Things that a man and a woman...'

But Rachel didn't hear the end of his cruel words. Unable to bear any more, she turned and fled, seeking the sanctuary of her own room as if all the devils in hell were after her.

To this day she could only be thankful that Greg and her mother hadn't woken. She would have been incapable of speech, unable to give any explanation of her distress if they had heard her and come to find out what was wrong...

Rachel stirred restlessly in her present-day bed. Simply recalling the events of that night hurt so badly that she felt as if the fine cream cotton of her duvet cover was as abrasive as sandpaper against her sensitised skin.

Harsh tears burned in her eyes, refusing her even the release of shedding them.

She had no idea how she had got through the following days. In one way, at least, Gabriel had made it easy for her. He'd rarely been in the house at all. When he hadn't been at work he'd been out somewhere, with Amanda presumably, and she'd hardly seen him to speak to.

Then, a fortnight after that appalling night, he'd had one last violent argument with his father and moved out. She had only had to endure one last dreadful confrontation with him before he'd been gone, moving out of her life for good, she had believed.

Slowly, gradually she had learned to adjust, to bury the past, but now events had brought him back into her world and it seemed it would all have to be done again.

The suitcase was the first thing Rachel saw when she came back into the house late the following afternoon.

It stood against the wall at the foot of the main staircase, the sight stopping her dead as she came into the house. For a second, as she stared at it, she felt as if she had been dragged back in time to that day two weeks after her birthday. Then, in the tangle of emotions that had filled her, relief had been the uppermost. Now she was no longer anything like as sure as she had been then.

'What does this mean?'

The question was jolted from her as Gabriel came down the stairs with a slim leather briefcase which he placed beside the other bag.

'As you can see, I'm leaving.'

'Leaving?' Her thoughts reeled under the impact of those two devastating words. 'But why? Where?'

'I'm going back to America.'

His statement was cool and distant as his expression, those deep eyes shuttered against her. He had only answered the second half of her question, she noted.

'*Why*?' she persisted. 'Is it because of the will?'

She had barely taken it in yet herself.

She knew that immediately after the wedding Greg had called his solicitor to his bedside and had changed his will, with nurses acting as witnesses. But all she had anticipated was that there would be a division of his property between his new wife and his son. So she had been stunned to find that *she* had received an equal share in what amounted to a three-way split.

'The will?' Gabriel's laughter was harsh, splintering the air around him. 'That was only what I expected.'

'Then you're not angry that I got the design studio?' Along with a sizeable personal allowance that would allow her to live in comfort for the rest of her life.

'Oh, Rachel…'

This time his laugh was softer, deeply sardonic, somehow even harder to bear than the harshness of a moment earlier.

'If you truly think that, then you just don't know me at all. I'm *glad* you got what you did. If you must know, I think you deserve it—and more—both you and your mother. You earned it by loving the stubborn old man in spite of everything—even when I'd given up on him.'

'He wasn't that difficult to love.'

'Oh, yes, he was.' Gabriel's mouth twisted wryly. 'And if he hadn't left you what was your right in his will, then I would have had to make the necessary arrangements myself. There's only—'

Hastily he caught himself up, obviously deciding not to complete the sentence.

'But it's better this way. I'm happy for you, Rachel.'

He sounded totally sincere. 'Then why go?'

'We agreed it would be better if I left quickly.'

'We did?'

I agreed to nothing, a pained inner voice cried. *Nothing*!

'You told me in no uncertain terms that there was nothing between us.'

'But you don't have to—'

'Rachel,' Gabriel put in with resigned patience, 'I do have a business to run.'

Suddenly the thought of losing him again, of not seeing him for another four and a half years, perhaps for ever, was more than she could bear.

'Surely it can survive without you for a couple more days?'

'Rachel, no!'

'Is it what happened yesterday?' she asked urgently, knowing she didn't have to elaborate. 'Because if it is, then, like you said, we agreed that nothing would…'

'We agreed.' He nodded his dark head slowly. 'But I don't trust myself to keep to that.'

He couldn't have said anything more guaranteed to make her heart lurch on a weak flutter of uncontrollable hope, to quicken her breathing, send the blood rushing into her cheeks.

'Then don't go,' she murmured softly.

On an impulse she moved to him, sliding her arms around his narrow waist, refusing to allow herself to be put off by the way he stiffened, his head going back defensively. Those dark eyes were carefully shielded, hiding his thoughts from her.

'Rachel…' This time her name was used as a warning.

It was a deterrent she chose to ignore. Somehow, out of the pain and confusion of the past, had come a new resolution, a new certainty, a new strength.

In spite of all that had happened, she still felt something for this man. She wanted him, but this time with the mature desire a grown woman feels. And every feminine instinct she possessed screamed the fact that he felt the same way towards her, though for some reason he was determined to resist it.

'Don't go,' she whispered, lifting luminous silver eyes to his shuttered face. 'Please don't go.'

'No, Rachel. I told you, this isn't going to happen…'

His very calmness, the measured control with which he removed her arms and turned away, was like a violence to her soul. She had seen that sort of control once before, and it had desolated her then too.

And now, when she was least able to bear it, the recollection of that other time came back to her. She saw him then, four and a half years earlier when—as now—with his flight booked, his bags packed, he had paused at the last minute to ask one final, brutal question.

'What happened between us, Rachel—I'm not usually so careless. Can I take it there will be no consequences from my foolish lack of control?'

Consequences. If she'd needed any further indication of his true feelings about the night they'd had sex together—because she refused to honour what had happened with the description of making love—then that had been it.

What to her would have been a child conceived in love, to him would have been an awkward, inconvenient problem—something to be dealt with as swiftly, efficiently and unemotionally as he handled the everyday decisions of his business world.

'If you mean am I pregnant,' she returned, her lips stiff from holding back the pain she wouldn't let him see, 'then, no, I'm not.'

She'd have said the same even if she had been carrying his child, just to spite him. But it was the truth, and she didn't know whether she was desperately sorry, simply relieved, or downright glad that their night together would have no unforeseen repercussions.

'Thank God!' he breathed, so fervently that she winced away from the anguish of hearing it.

'Why thank Him, Gabriel?' she flung at him, her tongue savage with bitterness. 'Because now you're free to be with your new mistress? With the woman you really wanted all the—?'

'*New mistress*!' Gabriel echoed cynically, and she knew his tone was meant to convey the message that if she had ever had the audacity to give herself the title of 'mistress' then she had been terribly mistaken.

She hadn't even meant so little to him. She hadn't been anything lasting, however briefly, in his life at all. All he had wanted from her was a sordid one night stand—the result of what he had termed his 'foolish lack of control'.

In the heat of the moment she had perhaps given him a few short moments of physical pleasure—if, in fact, she'd done that. After all, her innocence must have made her responses less passionate and uninhibited, less exciting than he was used to. When compared to women of the world, like Amanda, she must have been a terrible disappointment to him.

'No way!'

To her horror she realised that she had actually spoken her thoughts out loud.

'You're a very sensual young lady, Rachel, and one day you'll bring some lucky man a great deal of—'

Abruptly his words were bitten off, his face closing up so that she had no hope of reading what he had been about to say.

'And if we're talking about freedom,' he continued on a very different note, 'then the same applies to you. You'll be able to choose any man you want...'

Not true, a weak, despairing voice inside her head cried bitterly. *Not true*!

How could it ever be so when the only man she had ever wanted was here, in front of her? When he had just declared that he considered their relationship to have been no more than a 'foolish lack of control'.

'Now that you've initiated me into the art of sex, you mean? Oh, yes, I'll be able to pass on all you taught me to some other *lucky man*!'

She had the meagre satisfaction of seeing his eyes close momentarily, as if in distress at the crudeness of her words. But only a second later they were wide open again, and blazing harshly into hers.

'I hope to hell you respect yourself more than that!'

'Rather hypocritical, coming from you, don't you

think? It's too late to start playing the responsible adult all over again.'

His eyes were the only colour in his face. His skin was stretched tight across the strongly carved bones, his mouth rigid with control except for one corner where a tiny muscle jerked.

'Too late,' he agreed flatly. 'Way too late. But a word of warning, Rachel. If you can't think of me as just an acquaintance in future, then don't think of me at all. In fact, you'd do much better to forget me completely.'

She'd tried. Dear God, she'd tried! But it seemed that nothing would erase him from her mind. Here she was, four and a half years later, and nothing had eased the pain. She still felt exactly the way she had before.

Lifting her chin determinedly, she swallowed hard, directing her burning gaze to the back of Gabriel's averted head.

'This isn't going to happen,' she echoed bleakly. 'Why don't you tell me the truth, Gabriel? Admit that it never *was*. You never felt anything, did you?'

The accusation brought him swinging round to face her.

'Oh, God, Rachel, no!'

His choked cry, the look of shock on his face, should have gone some way to appeasing some of the anguish in her outraged heart. It should have been a part, at least, of the words of regret and apology she had longed to hear him say. But, strangely, it seemed to have exactly the opposite effect to the one she might have imagined.

Instead of reassuring her, it stirred up the silt of her nightmares, bringing to the surface the thoughts she had tried to suppress for so long.

'I mean, that night...I never expected you would respond as you did.'

The faintly bruised, bleak humour in Gabriel's voice and eyes tore at her already desolated heart.

'You took me unawares. We both weren't exactly sober, and I didn't quite know what had hit me.'

'That night,' Rachel echoed, not knowing whether she preferred the fact that his actions had been a greedy, opportunistic loss of control rather than a callous and deliberate seduction. 'And later?'

Something changed in his expression. Not so much a flinch, more a swift, instinctively defensive blink that she almost missed. It was only afterwards that she realised it had been used to conceal something. Something that had been in his eyes a moment before but which had been hastily erased.

'Later...?' she persisted, even though her heart cried out against the torture she was inflicting on it.

She knew that the answer to the question had the potential to bring even more devastating pain, but still she had to ask it.

'What about the night of my party, Gabriel? The time with Amanda? Was that something else you did when you "weren't exactly sober"?' She emphasised the quote venomously. 'Another time when you "didn't quite know what" had hit you?'

'No.'

It was low, flat and lifeless, accompanied by a vehement shake of his dark head.

'I knew exactly what I was doing then.'

Even though she'd forced him to tell her, Rachel still couldn't believe she'd heard the words. She didn't want to have heard them, and as he admitted the truth her heart tried desperately to reject it.

It couldn't be real! She wouldn't let it be! It was more than she could bear.

'You knew...'

She had tried to penetrate his mental armour, get through to whatever it was he was hiding from her. Instead it seemed that all she had done was totally destroy her own defences. She had no protection left against him, against the pain he could inflict on her, nothing to shield her from the white-hot agony inflicted by every word he spoke.

'Tell me the truth, Gabriel.'

'It is the bloody truth!'

He swung away violently, hands pushed deep into his trouser pockets as he stared out through the window.

'No!'

She wanted to lift her hands to her ears to blot out the sound of his voice and the hateful things he was telling her, but she forced them down to her sides again with a desperate effort.

'Tell me it isn't real—that it wasn't how it seemed! Tell me it was all just a set-up, that she came to your room…'

'As you did?'

It was a struggle to ignore his savage interjection, but she managed it—just. It was either that or collapse totally, admitting he had defeated her once and for all.

'Tell me you were drunk—or asleep…'

She knew she was clutching at straws, but without their fragile support she would definitely be going down for the third time, with the icy waters of despair closing over her defenceless head.

'Tell me I got there at just the wrong moment,' she pleaded. 'Another second or two and you would have realised what she was up to and told her to go—get out…'

Please tell me that. That, or any other explanation, however improbable, that I can try my hardest to believe!

As her words died away there was a pause. A long, thoughtful pause so charged with tension that she thought her overstretched nerves would actually snap under the strain. Gabriel's breath hissed in between his teeth as he slowly turned back to face her. His skin was stretched so tightly over his bones that it was white with tension.

'It's a tempting fantasy,' he said coldly. 'But, no, I can't lie to you.'

Rachel felt as if she had been punched with brutal

force right in the pit of her stomach. She had to gather all her strength around her before she could speak.

'Then, what…?'

'It was *exactly* as it seemed.' Each word was enunciated with freezing precision. 'It wasn't a set-up, and in no way was I the innocent party. In fact, I was the instigator of the whole damn thing—the prime mover, so to speak.'

The blackly cynical twist to his mouth became more pronounced.

'I could never claim that I was drunk. I may have tried to drink myself senseless that night, but unfortunately I remained stone-cold sober. And I wasn't even remotely taken advantage of.'

This time Rachel did lift her hands to cover her ears, but Gabriel reached out and pulled them down again, forcing her to listen. His calm, emotionless recital of the facts pounded against her head with the appalling force of hammer blows.

'Amanda wasn't "up to" anything, but I was. It was all real, angel, totally and completely real. Oh, Rachel…'

A gentle forefinger reached out and touched her cheek, coming away with a single tear on its tip. A tear she hadn't even been aware of having shed.

'I'm not worth this, sweetheart, believe me—not worth it at all. I left you and went straight to her in the space of just a couple of days, and I'd do it again tomorrow if the same situation arose. That's why I had to leave—go to America—then. And it's why I have to go back there, why I'm leaving right now.'

Dropping her hands, he turned on his heel, snatching up his bags and marching out of the house, not even sparing her a backward glance.

And it was as she heard his car door slam and the engine roar into life that Rachel felt the final blow fall.

Now she knew why it had mattered. Why she had asked, begged Gabriel for some sort of explanation. She still loved him and had done so for the past four and a half years. In spite of all the pain, the disgust, the belief that she hated him, the truth was that she had never stopped loving him and now she knew she never would.

CHAPTER EIGHT

ONE fifteen.

Automatically Rachel checked her watch again, frowning as she did so.

It was so unlike Gabriel to be late. Particularly when he had arranged the meeting. After twelve months of almost total silence from him, his sudden invitation to her to join him here, in New York, had been totally unexpected. But then, she was discovering quite a few things that were different about his lifestyle here in America.

The apartment, for one. When she had been expecting something neat and compact, like the attic rooms at home, the size and space of the place where Gabriel lived, with its amazing view of Central Park, had taken her breath away.

She hadn't anticipated that he would move out, either. That he would leave the place to her for the duration of her stay. If she'd known he'd planned on doing any such thing, she would have insisted on taking a room in an hotel.

'Sorry I'm late.'

A familiar voice broke into her thoughts as the subject of them touched her briefly on the shoulder before dropping into a chair on the opposite side of the restaurant table.

'Last-minute crisis as I was leaving the office. You found the place all right, then?'

'No trouble at all.'

It was a struggle to concentrate on her words. She had been unprepared for the heart-stopping impact of seventy-five inches of sexually devastating male in a light grey silk suit and immaculate white shirt that were the perfect complement to his dark hair and eyes, strong frame, wide shoulders and narrow hips.

Looks like his should carry a health warning, she reflected ruefully. Even knowing that he felt nothing for her couldn't stop her from indulging the hunger that twelve months without him had induced. Her eyes devoured the sight of him greedily; she wanted to fill the emptiness his absence had left in her life.

'The instructions you left were perfectly clear. Only an idiot would have got lost.'

'And we both know you're very far from being an idiot.' He lifted a hand to summon a waiter to their table. 'Another drink?'

'No, thanks. I've barely touched this.'

And she felt jittery enough already, simply seeing him. She had learned her lesson in the past. Alcohol and Gabriel Tiernan were a lethal combination.

'You're looking well,' Gabriel continued once his wine had been brought. 'Very glamorous, in fact. I like the hair.'

'Thank you.' Rachel smoothed a self-conscious hand over the sleek shoulder-length style. 'It took a bit of adjusting to, but I'm getting used to it.'

'What made you decide to get it cut?'

'Oh, you know—I wanted a change of image.'

She wasn't going to admit to the truth, which was that when he had returned to America she had resolved to get her life back under control, starting with an overhaul of her appearance.

It hadn't worked, of course. Chopping six inches off her hair wasn't likely to make her forget that Gabriel had ever existed. Nor was a brand-new wardrobe. But at least it had given her something else to think about, and the new hairstyle, together with the elegantly tailored cream suit she wore today, had given her self-confidence a much needed boost.

'I thought I'd looked like Alice in Wonderland for much too long.'

'I quite liked the Alice look.'

For a second, as the dark chocolate gleam of his eyes rested on the burnished colour of her hair, she felt a sensation like the trail of icy fingers slide over her skin at the back of her neck.

'All men like long hair,' she managed shakily, nerves twisting sharply as a sudden frown drew his dark brows together.

'You've lost weight too. Was that deliberate?'

'I wasn't pining for you, if that's what you were implying!'

'Of course not,' Gabriel returned smoothly. 'Would you like to order now?'

The speed with which the staff of the restaurant responded to his signal left Rachel with no alternative but to do just that. She forced her attention to the menu with an effort that left her feeling as if she had just done a couple of rounds with a heavyweight boxer rather than perform the simple task of selecting a meal from the extensive choice in front of her.

'I lost some weight when I had flu,' she conceded once they were alone again, referring to the illness that had kept her in bed during his one brief visit to London during the past year, for his father's memorial service.

At the time she hadn't known whether she was glad or sorry that she had been too unwell to see him. She had longed for just a sight of his face, but had known intuitively that, as now, it would only waken old, aching yearnings that were better kept hidden.

It had been on that visit that Gabriel had seen the designs she had been working on and bought them all for his American company. That, in its turn, had led to his unexpected suggestion that she might like to visit New York to see them actually made up.

'I've been so busy since then that I never had the chance to put it back on.'

'So how are you now? And your mother?'

The stiff formality of the question riled her, coming so close after the recollection of how determinedly he had kept away from her during his time in London. She hadn't been *that* ill.

'Much you care!'

'As a matter of fact, I do.'

'Is that the truth? Then why haven't you visited more often, or at least phoned?' She was too much on edge now to care that she had come close to contradicting her own declaration that she hadn't missed him.

'You know why.'

Gabriel's face had closed up, and he reached for his glass again with a movement that was so smooth, so forcefully controlled that it made Rachel wonder if that effect had been exactly what he had aimed at.

'I thought it was for the best.'

'You thought! *You* thought! Did you ever give any consideration to anyone other than yourself?'

'Frequently.' It was totally inflexionless, all emotion ironed out. 'But I still decided that my way of handling things was for the best.'

'I'll just bet you did!'

The memory of the sleepless nights, the long, lonely days she had endured in his absence piqued her, driving her to want to hurt as she was hurting. She couldn't bear to think that he had found it so easy to put her completely from his mind when she had never spent a single day without some thought of him.

'You never wanted Mum and I to inherit any part of the business, and so now you just hate being tied to us because of it.'

That got a reaction. And not one she was comfortable with either. She had to fight not to flinch back fearfully as Gabriel sat up straighter in his chair, anger flaring in the depths of his eyes.

'You know damn well that's light years away from the truth! For one thing, seeing as I'm still a major shareholder in Tiernan's, I'd have been a fool to abandon all interest in the way it was run.'

His hand closed over his wine glass so forcefully that Rachel was forced to wonder whether he wished it was her neck.

'After all, your mother has no experience in business matters whatsoever. But everything seems to be going well. Share prices might have looked a little uncertain just after Dad died, but they've recovered now.'

The hand that had clenched around his glass relaxed again, but with such an obvious effort that it was clear he had almost had to force himself to do it.

'And obviously I know how well *you*'ve been doing.'

'So you've been spying on me!'

A resigned sigh greeted her antagonistic remark.

'Are you determined to take everything I say the wrong way? I make it my business to know how every section of Tiernan's is doing. That is why you're here. What did you think about what you saw this morning?'

The transition was so smooth, so seamless, that for a second or two Rachel didn't even realise it had happened. By the time she registered that she had been led onto a very different topic it was too late to protest. It would have looked petty to revive the argument of moments before.

And with typical Gabriel cleverness he had steered the conversation onto a subject he knew she couldn't help but be enthusiastic about.

'It was wonderful!' she declared honestly. 'I love what you've done over here. It's no wonder T2 is such a success. And that display...'

Words deserted her as she recalled the feeling of sheer excitement she had felt to see a whole window full of her own designs in the Fifth Avenue shop. Luckily the arrival of their starters gave her a chance to collect her thoughts.

'Thank you for giving my work such a boost,' she said simply.

'I'm not the one who deserves the credit for it,' Gabriel returned easily, meeting her eyes across the table. 'That goes to you. After all, it's your talent that created such beautiful jewellery. I would have been a fool *not* to give them that sort of prominence. You must have seen the effect they have. Very few women can walk past without stopping to look.'

He lifted his glass in a silent but eloquent toast that started a glow of delight deep in her heart.

'And when they look they fall in love with a necklace or a pair of earrings that they *must* have. Even the men are attracted. All they can think of is how wonderful one of those pieces would look around their wife's throat, or on a lover's hand...'

'I'm glad you're pleased.'

Rachel had to speak in order to shatter the hypnotic spell Gabriel had been weaving. His husky tones seemed to have coiled around her thoughts like smoke, driving everything else from her mind and holding her mesmerised. All she could see were his eyes, all she could hear was his voice. The sense of his words had blurred into incomprehension, becoming just sound that played over her skin like a gentle breeze.

'More than pleased.'

Gabriel's smile was slow and warm.

'You must know you're a star. You have a spectacular, magnificent talent. That's why I wanted you to come over here, so that you can see for yourself how well your designs are selling.'

Only that? It stabbed painfully to realise that deep down some weak, foolish part of her heart had actually let itself believe—hope—that there could be something more.

Gabriel's fax, and the brief phone call with which he had followed it up, had offered purely business reasons for his suggestion that she visit New York. But only now did she acknowledge to herself that she had dreamed of some other, more personal interest in her trip.

'But that isn't the only reason I invited you over.'

'It isn't?'

It was almost as if he had read her thoughts, or seen the pain of them in her eyes. And now it was impossible to suppress the lift of her heart in response to a new gleam of hope as her head came up, the light of excitement in her eyes.

'I have two pieces of news for you; one personal, one about work. Work first—I have a commission for you—something really special.'

The food, that only moments before had tasted so wonderful, now turned to ashes in her mouth. She felt as if she was dying inside, the anguish made all the worse by the split second of hope that had preceded it.

'A commission?' she said, trying to inject a note of enthusiasm into her voice as she pushed her plate away from her, losing all interest in her meal. 'Tell me about it.'

'Not yet.'

His smile was mysterious and teasing. At least her subterfuge had convinced him. He believed that her interest was in the work he offered, the challenge to her design skills.

'Tell me a little bit about yourself first. About what you've been doing these past twelve months—apart from work, that is. Is there a man in your life these days?'

Renewed pain kicked at her heart.

'Didn't your spies tell you that?' she flung at him, hoping he would take the flare of distress in her eyes for defiance.

'Not spies, Rachel,' he said gently. 'And they only report on the business. My—sources—didn't tell me anything about your private life.'

'Oh, so you know nothing of the queues of men lining up outside the house, just begging me to have dinner with them?'

She aimed for airy insouciance but didn't know whether she had succeeded or missed it by a mile as she saw his dark eyes fasten on her face and the strange half-smile that barely curved his lips.

'I can believe that,' he said quietly.

'You can?'

Once more she had cause to be grateful for the arrival of the waiter, giving her another chance to collect her thoughts. She hoped that the few minutes' grace needed to clear away one course and serve another might push the disturbing topic from Gabriel's mind, but as soon as they were alone he returned to it once more.

'You sounded surprised. Why should it be so amazing that I should think—know—you must be attractive to many men? And is there one special man amongst them?'

Instinct warned Rachel that it was a loaded question. Her thoughts were pulled back to the last time they had been together, recalling painfully the way he had told her she was free to be with any man she wanted.

'One exclusive lover?' Hastily she reverted to the careless tone of moments before. 'I can't say there is. Not anyone I'd want to settle down with, anyway.'

He hadn't liked something about her answer. But what? The word 'lover', or the fact that she had deliberately made her comment ambiguous? It could be taken to imply that there were, as she had declared, dozens of would-be suitors—or none at all.

In fact the cruel truth was that she had *tried*, really tried. In the months since she had last seen him, she had accepted almost every date that had been offered. She had been to many places with an assortment of different men in an attempt to drive all thought of Gabriel from her mind.

It had all been in vain. She had spent all her time comparing her current escort with Gabriel—all unfavourably. No one had ever come close, and she knew they never would.

'I think I'll just stick to playing the field.'

That comment was like adding fuel to an already blazing fire. A dark scowl crossed his face, and he stabbed his knife into his food with a force that spoke of controlled aggression, a burning temper only just reined in.

'You want to be careful, Rachel...'

In contrast to his actions, his words were as smooth as silk, but the ebony eyes held an ominous glitter that she was afraid to interpret too closely. She only knew that it set her mental antennae quivering, alert to potential danger in the air.

'That sort of lifestyle is neither wise nor healthy in today's sexual climate. And a talent like yours is too precious to lose.'

A talent! The word slashed at her brutally, deeply undermining her already shaky composure. Was that all he would regret losing if she was no longer around?

And what gave him the right to think that he could walk out of her life, as he had done a year ago, declaring he wanted nothing to do with her, and then stroll back into it whenever he chose? Making critical comments about the way he believed she was living her life, what was more!

'I'll live my life my own way, Gabriel,' she told him stiffly. 'It's none of your business how—'

'Promiscuity is never an admirable trait,' Gabriel inserted sharply, and even though she'd deliberately led him to thinking this way his comment stung her into impetuous speech.

'And hypocrisy is? Strikes me there's a heavy suggestion of pots and kettles and the colour black about the way you're talking, brother dear. Tell me, do you still go through women as quickly as you did when you were at home?'

She didn't have to elaborate to clarify exactly what she meant. The echo of the pain she had felt still rang in her voice, even after an interval of more than five years.

'I knew exactly what I was doing!'

'And I didn't?'

Rachel no longer cared that her raised voice had attracted the attention of other diners nearby. She was incensed, her attention focused so strongly on the man before her that the whole restaurant could have been staring and she wouldn't have noticed.

'You were only nineteen.' It was some gratification that Gabriel at least looked distinctly uncomfortable.

'And didn't have a brain in my head? It wouldn't occur to you to take responsibility for what happened between us?'

The dark eyes never faltered, his unwavering stare twisting her nerves into tight, painful knots.

'Believe me, I've lived with the responsibility, the regret, ever since.'

Regret. He really knew how to put the knife in. How to push it in as far as it would go and give it a nasty twist for good measure.

'I should have realised that you were rather more drunk than I—'

'Drunk! Oh, so now it's the drink that was to blame!'

The bitter realisation that what he regretted was the fact that he had slept with her at all, and not his callous behaviour afterwards, was more than she could bear. The single night that she had spent with him had been the most wonderful, the happiest time of her life. But with a single brutal stroke he had destroyed that too.

'It was nothing to do with an adult taking advantage—'

'*Taking advantage*!'

Gabriel's voice hadn't been raised above conversational level, but the way the words had whistled through his teeth, his skin tightly drawn over the strong bones of his face, etching white lines around his nose and mouth, warned how close he was to losing control. But still she couldn't stop.

'Well, what else would you call it? You've admitted I was barely nineteen—and tiddly. And we both know you wrote the book on manipulation. You've made an art form out of getting women to do exactly as you want while keeping them in the palm of your hand.'

'Is that a fact?'

If there had been danger in his voice before, then this cold, clear enunciation of every syllable was like the sound of a cruel trap closing over a defenceless animal.

'And what page of this book do you claim that *you* are on? *You* weren't manipulated. If I recall correctly, you were only too willing. You made the first move, led me on. I gave you every chance to say no. A chance you never took.'

'Of course not. That's because…'

Rachel froze mid-sentence, horrified by what she had almost let slip in the heat of the moment.

Because I love you she had been about to say. She had come close to opening her heart to him, letting him see the precious, vulnerable secret that lay hidden inside it, exposing it to his darkly cynical gaze, his scathing contempt.

Because I love you was exactly what she was *not* supposed to say.

The love she felt for him was one of the complications he had declared she trailed after her, threatening to entangle him and drag him down. Love that demanded faithfulness and commitment, that wasn't just a one-night stand, a physical affair that could be ended as soon as he became bored. It was the last thing that he wanted from her.

'Because you…?' Gabriel prompted huskily when she remained tongue-tied, unable to think of anything to fill the sudden silence left by her uncompleted sentence. 'Tell me.'

But Rachel's mind had blown a fuse. There was nothing she could say. Nothing that would not incriminate her, or make him turn away, rejecting her completely. Panic-stricken silver eyes locked with deep brown as she struggled to think.

But then her rescue came from a totally new and unexpected source.

'Gabriel...'

A new voice sounded somewhere above her downbent head. A female voice, young and light, with a soft American accent. It also held a touch of uncertainty, a hesitation that spoke of feelings very carefully controlled.

'Cassie! Hi!'

Gabriel's immediate switch from Crown Prosecutor mode to relaxed, warm friendship was so startling that it jerked Rachel's head up in a rush. She almost groaned aloud at the sight that met her eyes.

Oh, Lord, this was all she needed! Amanda Bryant reborn, or at the very least her double!

The girl who had come to their table was tall and model-slim, luxuriant black hair falling in carefully contrived waves around a heart-shaped face. She was beautiful too, with high cheekbones, wide brown eyes and a soft, full mouth.

Gabriel was already on his feet, one hand going out to draw the newcomer to him as he pressed a soft kiss on her cheek.

'I wasn't expecting you quite so soon.'

His tone was warm, rich with an affection that made Rachel feel as if she was slowly starving to death deep inside. Once she had been on the receiving end of that sort of gentleness, but it had shrivelled and died, and could never be reincarnated.

'I know I'm early. I'm sorry if I interrupted your conversation.'

This woman was *jealous*, Rachel noted with a sense of shock. It was there in the undertone to her words, in every swift, uncertain glance at Gabriel, at Rachel's own face.

And that hand on Gabriel's arm was definitely proprietorial. She might just as well have stuck a label saying 'Hands off! This man is mine!' on one lapel of that superbly tailored suit. With a sharp stab of distress Rachel was forced to acknowledge that she recognised the symptoms so easily because they were the ones she suffered from too.

'Won't you introduce me?' she said pointedly.

'Of course.'

Gabriel's smile was easy and relaxed, and as he turned back to Rachel he slid his hand into Cassie's, curling his long fingers securely around her elegantly manicured ones in a gesture of reassurance.

'I said I had some news for you. I was only waiting for Cassie to arrive before I told you. Cass, this is Rachel Amis, the designer I told you about. And, Rachel, I'd like you to meet Cassie Elliot…'

Suddenly Rachel was deeply grateful she was sitting down. Something in Gabriel's tone told her exactly what was coming, and she strongly suspected that if she had been on her feet her legs would have given way beneath her.

Two pieces of news, he had said. One personal, one about work. Oh, God, no! Please let it not be that. Let it be *anything* but that!

But even as she sent up the desperate, silent prayer Cassie moved to place her left hand over the one Gabriel had so closely entwined with hers. There was no way that Rachel could avoid the gleam of the brilliant diamond in the ring she wore, its cold, bright blaze burning away all trace of hope. Dimly, through the roaring inside her head, she heard Gabriel confirm her fears.

'Cassie is my fiancée. I asked her to marry me just over a month ago and, to my delight, she accepted. The wedding will be in London in six weeks' time.'

CHAPTER NINE

'BUT why London?'

Lydia's question echoed the only coherent one Rachel had been able to frame in the chaos of her devastated thoughts after Gabriel's announcement.

She had choked out a form of congratulation in a voice that had had neither substance nor sincerity, but after that rationality had caved in. She had only been able to concentrate on what was to her the worst possible aspect of this coming wedding, after the announcement itself.

'I mean, why not New York, where they both live?'

Rachel had asked herself that over and over in the three weeks since that fateful meeting. Why, if Gabriel had to marry, did he have to come to London to do it?

Wasn't it bad enough that he had met someone—someone *else*—fallen in love with them, asked them to be his wife, without knowing that she would have to endure the ceremony taking place on her own doorstep, so to speak?

'Apparently Cassie's mother lives in London, and Cassie herself was born here. The family went out to America when she was barely six months old, but when her father died Mrs Elliot came back here. She's recently married again herself, so technically she's Mrs Keaton now. The wedding's to be from her house.'

Which meant that she wouldn't even have the excuse that New York was too far to travel for what wasn't exactly a family wedding, Rachel acknowledged with silent misery. Only that morning the invitations had arrived, confirming the unwelcome details.

'I wouldn't have thought that you'd want to go.'

It was a last-ditch attempt to provide herself with some justification for refusing. But, surprisingly, Lydia seemed to be delighted at the prospect of Gabriel's approaching marriage. She even appeared prepared to forget the long-standing feud between herself and her stepson.

'I wouldn't miss it for the world! It sounds as if everyone who's anyone will be there. I've told Gabriel he can use this house as a base...'

'You've done *what*?'

Rachel's head reeled. If there was one thing that could make things even worse, it was this. Just to imagine Gabriel staying in the house in the days before his wedding was unbearable, so how could she endure the reality? And how could she watch him walk out of here, on his way to marry Cassie?

'Mum, you haven't! You can't!'

'I can and I have. It was what Greg would have wanted, Rachel, and really this is still Gabriel's home.'

'But you and he...'

'I'm willing to put our past problems behind us.'

Lydia, who was on her way out for the evening, picked up her handbag and began checking through it, making sure her keys and her credit cards were in the right place.

'We resolved them months ago, when he was over here for the memorial service. In fact, if I'd known how he tried to persuade his father to marry me much earlier in our relationship then things could have been more civilised from the start.'

'He tried to persuade Greg to marry you? *Gabriel*?' Rachel couldn't believe she had heard right. 'But he was totally against it.'

'At first, yes.'

Moving to the mirror over the mantelpiece, Lydia considered her appearance, smoothing a dark strand of hair back from her forehead.

'But it seemed he changed his mind. Apparently that

was one of the reasons why he left for America in the first place. They fell out very badly over it.'

'But he said that was about the business!'

'Quite possibly it was over that as well.'

After applying a careful coat of lip-colour, Lydia nodded her satisfaction as she dropped the gold tube into her bag and clicked it shut.

'Gabriel has treated me very fairly since his father died. He never challenged the changes in the will when he might well have done if he'd wanted to. After all...'

She coloured faintly, her eyes suddenly bright with unshed tears.

'Technically, Greg and I never consummated our marriage. And for the past year he's practically been running Tiernan's as well as T2—almost doubling the profits in the process. And now that he's getting married...'

It sounded almost as if it was the marriage that had finally swayed her mother's opinion in Gabriel's favour. And perhaps he had suspected something of the sort, Rachel reflected, recalling his declaration a year before that before his father died he'd had no intention of setting foot inside the house again until he was married.

But it seemed uncharacteristically prudish of Lydia who had, after all, lived for seven years with the man she loved without worrying about a formal ceremony.

The man she loved. The thought made Rachel want to double up in pain, folding her arms tightly around her body as if to hold herself together. Would she have been able to follow her mother's example and commit herself to Gabriel without the promise of marriage?

Even as she asked herself the question she knew there was no doubt in her mind. She would have sold her soul to be with him, whatever the circumstances.

But now, of course, she would never get the chance. He had chosen Cassie to share his life in the future.

Face it, she told herself sternly. He *loves* someone else. You don't even figure in his life.

'Anyway, he'll be arriving tonight. You will be here to welcome him, won't you?'

'Tonight?' She had hoped for a little more time to adjust. 'Do I have to? I mean, won't you be here?'

'I'm meeting Pamela. We're going to that new musical, and then I'm spending the weekend at her home. I *did* tell you, Rachel!'

Vaguely Rachel recollected her mother mentioning something of the sort, but she had been so shell-shocked with the news of Gabriel's impending marriage that nothing really registered these days.

'I'll be back on Monday.' A brief peck on her daughter's cheek, and then she headed for the door. 'Have fun!'

Fun was the last thing she expected to have. How could she anticipate Gabriel's arrival with anything other than dread?

And yet, even as she acknowledged that fact, a weak, masochistic part of her heart was also admitting to a foolish longing to see him again. She even found herself checking her appearance in the same mirror her mother had used, wishing she had worn something a little more flattering than the plain denim jeans and white T-shirt.

The sound of a car door slamming outside came so soon after her mother's departure that she assumed Lydia had forgotten something and come back to fetch it. But the ringing of the doorbell shattered that hope, setting her nerves jangling with the realisation that there was only one person it could be.

The walk across the hall felt as if someone had strewn the tiled floor with broken glass that splintered even more as she walked, stabbing sharply with every step she took.

'You could have used your key!' she declared as she stood aside to let Gabriel inside. 'I take it you still have one?'

It didn't come out as she had intended, sounding abrasive and confrontational instead, and to judge from the cynical twist to his mouth that was how Gabriel interpreted it too.

'And good evening to you too,' he drawled satirically. 'Of course I have a key, but as this is your mother's house now I thought it was more polite to ring instead.'

It was a perfectly valid reason, but to Rachel, in her present hypersensitive state, it sounded like a way of underlining the fact that since his father's death she and Gabriel were no longer even remotely connected. The tenuous link that had bound them together had ceased to exist, and with it had gone even a pretence at a relationship.

'Well, it might have been more *polite* to consider who had to answer the door. My mother's out and it's Mrs Reynolds' night off.'

Oh, why couldn't she stop? She was making matters so much worse with every word that nervous tension drove from her mouth.

'I'm so sorry you had to come all the way across the hall simply to let me in.' The mockery was darker now, the deep brown eyes reflecting no trace of humour. 'But now that you've done your duty you can go back to whatever you were doing or whoever you were doing it with and leave me to fend for myself.'

'No, it's all right.'

Giving herself a firm mental shake, she hastily pulled her thoughts together.

'I wasn't doing anything important, and I promised Mum I'd look after you. Have you eaten yet? Because if not I could make you some supper.'

'*You* will?'

Gabriel's look of horror was so spontaneous, so wryly humorous, that she knew exactly what he was thinking. It took her back six or more years, to the time when, as a teenager, she had first tried out her untrained culinary skills on him.

'It's all right. You're quite safe.'

Her own laughter in response was easy and unforced,

some of the tension leaving her as she found herself smiling naturally for the first time since he had arrived.

'I've come a long way since the concrete rock buns, not to mention the half-raw, half-burnt shepherd's pie. And besides, Mrs Reynolds keeps a very well-stocked freezer. Even I can't ruin defrost-and-heat stuff.'

'In that case I'll risk it.' His smile matched hers.

It was only when that warmth lit his face that she realised just how far it had been from his expression all this time.

He looked dreadful, she noticed. Even allowing for the rigours of transatlantic travel, the shadows under his eyes, the drained pallor of his cheeks, were surely the result of more than mere tiredness. He looked miles away from the traditional image of the happy bridegroom anticipating his wedding with joy and excitement.

But, whatever he looked like, she couldn't take her eyes off him. Even knowing he was committed to the delightful Cassie didn't stop the hunger from permeating every cell, right through to her bones, at just the sight of him.

Like her, he was supremely casually dressed. But she was sure that her own clothes had nothing like the impact of the loose linen jacket, navy like his T-shirt, and well-worn denim jeans when combined with the lean, hard strength of the body beneath them.

'I'll just dump my bags in my room, then. I take it I am still in the same one? Rachel?'

'Oh, yes.' Rachel forced her thoughts away from the wanton path they were following. 'Same room. Have a shower if you want. There's no rush.'

Because the problem was that Cassie *was* delightful, she admitted to herself as she dragged her eyes away from the compelling length of his legs in the clinging denim, the taut lines of his shoulder and chest, forcing herself into the kitchen as he headed upstairs.

In the short space of time that she'd had to get to know the other woman in New York, she had taken to her at once. It would all have been so much easier if she could have hated her on sight, but instead she had positively liked her—more than liked her. Under any other circumstances she would have approved of Gabriel's choice of bride—or if Cassie had been marrying any other man.

But Cassie was the woman Gabriel was going to marry. In three weeks, they would be man and wife, and she had always to remember that.

With that in mind, the first thing she said when Gabriel reappeared in the kitchen was, 'Is Cassie with you?'

'She flew over with me, but then I dropped her off at her mother's house.'

He was helping himself to coffee from the filter machine on the worktop as he spoke.

'She's staying with Mrs Keaton until the big day, but there wasn't room for me. Besides, her mother is a dyed-in-the-wool traditionalist. The bride and the groom mustn't sleep under the same roof until after the wedding.'

'Of course not. And definitely no seeing the bride the night before!'

Rachel cursed her flippant tongue as her comment combined with a vivid mental image of just how beautiful Cassie would look in her wedding night finery, with Gabriel... Her vision blurred with tears, and it took several seconds' frantic blinking before she dared to risk continuing with the slicing of tomatoes for a salad.

'Definitely not that,' Gabriel agreed, a strange edge to his voice. 'Can I do anything to help?'

'It's well under control,' Rachel assured him, wishing the same could be said for her emotions.

She also wished that she'd never suggested the shower. For the past ten minutes her mind had been going wild, treating her to pictures of his lithe, masculine form slick with hot water, the foam from the shower gel cascading over his smooth, toned flesh.

And now that he was actually here it was no better. If anything, it was worse. Even though he was now dressed in a rich blue polo shirt and another, equally worn pair of denims, the clothes were no protection from the sensual direction of her uncontrolled thoughts.

His hair was still damp and curling softly over the base of his skull, and the soft denim clung like a second skin to the narrow waist and long legs. The warmth of the shower had eased some of the harsh, tired lines from his face, and just to look at him made a twist of reaction uncoil deep in her lower body.

'There's a chicken and mushroom pie, courtesy of Mrs Reynolds, but it still needs twenty minutes before it's ready. It depends on how hungry you are. There's some soup if you...'

A shake of his dark head stopped her in mid-flow.

'The pie will be fine. I can wait.'

'Well, then...'

The salad was finished and she was deprived of the practicalities she had been using as a diversion. Now she stood uncertainly, wiping her hands carefully on a cloth, not knowing how to proceed.

Gabriel took the initiative from her.

'Why don't I pour you one of these...?' He indicated his mug of coffee. 'Or perhaps something stronger, and we'll go through to the lounge until the food's ready.'

She would have preferred to find something more to do in the kitchen, but the pie was browning nicely in the oven, the vegetables were prepared, and there was nothing more needing attention for a while.

'Just coffee, then.'

He poured one for her, adding cream automatically, but discarded the unfinished half of his own drink into the sink.

'I think I'll go with the harder stuff,' he said wryly. 'I've been drinking coffee by the gallon on the plane and I feel totally wired on caffeine. Perhaps some alcohol might relax me.'

It was probably just the over-sensitised way she was feeling that made her imagine the way his hand hovered over the top of a bottle of champagne in the drinks cabinet before moving on to a less emotive red burgundy. This Gabriel, newly engaged and planning his wedding to his beautiful bride-to-be, would probably have no recollection of her memories of the sparkling wine, let alone any desire to revive them.

'So, are the preparations for the wedding in full swing?' she forced herself to ask, even though it was the last thing she wanted to talk about.

'If the way Cassie's head's been full of nothing but is any indication, then, yes, I should think you could say that. She was busy with endless lists all through the flight.'

'As her mother's such a traditionalist, I suppose it's going to be very formal?'

Gabriel's nod was abstracted, his dark-eyed gaze turned down into the ruby liquid in his glass as he seated himself opposite her.

'Half a dozen bridesmaids, pageboys, top hats and tails.'

There was a disturbing lack of enthusiasm in his checking off the 'ingredients' of a society wedding. But then men rarely took a great deal of interest in the intricate details of such things, Rachel told herself. She, however, was struggling with the effect on her breathing caused by the thought of his impressive form encased in the elegant tailoring of a formal morning suit.

'Flowers, invitations, food... It's never-ending.'

'Well, if there's anything I can do to help...'

Oh, *why* had she said that? The coffee she had never really wanted suddenly tasted sour in her mouth. Leaning forward to place the mug on the tiled hearth, she let a curtain of bronze hair fall forward to hide her betraying change of expression.

She didn't know how she was going to live with the fact that Gabriel was getting married, and she certainly didn't want to *help* him towards it. So it was with a dragging, aching pain deep inside that she saw his slow, thoughtful nod.

'Actually, there is something. Apart from my mother, Rachel, you're the only family I've got, so I'd like you to be part of the day. There's one thing I'd really like you to do for me.'

There was a note in his voice that brought her head up in a rush. 'Do *for me*,' he had said, feeding her the sudden weak, foolish hope that perhaps he wanted something she could give willingly, something that would show her love…

'You remember when you came to New York and I said I had two pieces of news? One of them was about your work, and I never got round to telling you any more about that because Cassie interrupted things and then the time was never right.'

Rachel made an inarticulate sound that he could take as agreement if he liked. She knew only too well why the time had never been 'right'. She had made damn sure that it wouldn't be.

From the moment that Gabriel had sprung on her the announcement of his engagement she had acted like an automaton. Not thinking, not functioning at all rationally, she had known only one thing. That she had to get out of there *fast*—before she gave herself away completely and let him, and his fiancée, whose suspicions had obviously already been aroused, see just how badly the news had affected her.

How she had managed it, she had no idea. But somehow she had smiled and made the right sort of congratulatory noises. Then she had mumbled some excuse about meeting friends and escaped. From then onwards she had filled what remained of her stay in America with work-related meetings, socialising, and even more meetings, never once letting herself and Gabriel be left alone together until it had been time to catch her flight home.

'You mentioned a commission. An important one.'

At his nod of agreement a spark of interest lit up in her eyes and she sat up straighter.

'For a major client?'

'You could say that. *I'd* be the one doing the commissioning. Rachel, I want you to design something very special for me.'

The liberating spark of interest had gone, doused by an icy rush of realism. Threaded through his words was an undertone that darkened his request, making it something of deeper, more disturbing significance.

Her blood chilled, slowed in her veins, and she knew the name he was going to speak even before he opened his mouth again.

'I'd love you to design something for Cassie. A very special piece of jewellery, something that would be my wedding present to her.'

'Never!'

The word was driven from her lips by the shock that had had the force of a violent blow to her heart, an agony of rejection she couldn't control.

'No way!'

'But you have the skill, the talent to make it something really spectacular. What do you think about a tiara, perhaps? Something to hold her veil—?'

'I said, *no way*!'

Create a piece of jewellery for his bride? Something to make Cassie look even more beautiful on the day she married him? He didn't know what he was asking.

How could she do anything to enhance the other woman's appearance when all she wanted was to be there, in her place, at his side?

'You're asking too much!'

Ebony eyes narrowed swiftly, and his frown seemed to be one of genuine confusion.

'But why? I would have thought it would be the perfect opportunity to win yourself some valuable publicity. Everyone at the wedding will see just how magnificent your work can be. It will be on all the society pages in the papers. You couldn't have a better chance to win yourself more customers. And I would have thought that, as family, you'd like to…'

'Like to!' Rachel echoed harshly. 'Like to be part of your wedding? Share your and Cassie's happiness? Do you really believe there could be anything I'd hate more after the way you—?'

'Oh, God!' he interjected, just in time to stop her from making a complete fool of herself with an admission of just how badly he'd hurt her. 'Rachel, no! Tell me it's not that! The last thing I wanted was to mess up your life…'

He looked sincere. He *sounded* sincere. He had even been able to inject an appropriate degree of concern into his expression, make it burn in his eyes.

'If I hurt you…'

'Hurt?'

Covering her tracks hastily, she managed a cynical laugh that sounded halfway convincing at least.

'Oh, no, that wasn't what I meant at all.'

If she'd aimed at knocking him off balance, then she'd certainly succeeded. His frown was one of frank confusion, and the fingers that raked through the dark sleekness of his hair were distinctly unsteady.

'Then what did you mean?'

Standing up suddenly, he moved to refill his glass. The uncharacteristic way his hand jerked, slopping a couple of drops of wine over the edge, tugged at something close to her heart. But she couldn't afford to let him see any weakness in her.

'If we're talking of my nineteenth birthday, then you were right when you said that was a mutual thing. A quick-burning hunger, easily aroused and just as easily appeased. But that—and even more so what happened afterwards—taught me one thing. It showed me how little such things matter. To all men, probably, but especially to you.'

The force of her feelings drove her to her feet. She felt better this way, facing him almost level. He was too intimidating, too overwhelming to cope with when towering over her as he had been before.

'Knowing that, how could I ever want to play a part in your wedding? How could I listen to you promise to love and honour someone until death do you part? It would make me sick!'

This is where it really gets painful, she told herself, as the force of her outburst died away into an uneasy silence. This is where he tells me that it might have been like that in the past, but with Cassie it will be different.

All he has to do is say that he feels more for her than he's ever felt for any other woman. That he *loves* her. And if he tells me that then I'll know it's real, because Gabriel never exaggerates, never tells anything other than the exact truth.

CHAPTER TEN

'I INTEND to make those vows very seriously,' Gabriel said, and it took the space of a couple of heartbeats before his actual words became clear in Rachel's mind.

Having nerved herself for the agony his declaration of love for Cassie would bring her, she was totally unprepared for the very different response she heard in its place. She also had to refocus her thoughts swiftly as she caught the bleakness of Gabriel's declaration, the emptiness in his eyes.

'And I mean to try to keep them. I won't make them easily, but I believe in what they say. I shall try to be the best husband I can be to Cassie, and that means being faithful to her alone for as long as we're together. Unfaithfulness in a husband is a moral crime in my book.'

'In a husband, perhaps, but not in a lover.' Rachel hid her hurt behind a mask of cynicism. 'Then there was no ring, no vows, so what was between us was just a casual, unimportant fling, easily dismissed.'

She saw the ominous warning of danger deep in his eyes before he actually reacted. The hand that held his glass tightened so fiercely that the fragile stem actually snapped beneath its cruel pressure. With a savage expletive he tossed it aside, watching with a terrifying indifference as it shattered on the marble hearth.

'Gabriel...' she began in protest, then lost the power of speech completely as he turned to her, his face suddenly haggard, skin drained of all colour and stretched so tight across his bones that it was almost translucent.

'If you think for one moment that you were "easily dismissed" then you don't have eyes in your head. If you believe that what there was between us was "unimportant", then you never experienced one iota of the emotions I did at the time.'

She almost thought she could believe him. It was obscene how much she *wanted* to believe him. And yet to do so would be the emotional equivalent of asking him to slit her throat with a very blunt knife.

'What I felt and what you did were two totally different things! In fact, I doubt if any part of how you behaved comes under the heading of *feelings*, except perhaps purely physical ones!'

'Damn you to hell, Rachel, you couldn't be more wrong! You haven't the faintest bloody idea what you're talking about!'

The terrible fury in his voice, the blaze in his eyes, his very stance, with his fists clenched hard at his sides, all put the fear of God into her. But she was determined not to let him see that.

'I couldn't be more *right*! I mean—tell me, did I *imagine* what happened afterwards? Did I imagine that Amanda Bryant was in your bed? Was she just a fiction, a mirage?'

'No...'

'No. And you can't claim that it wasn't as it seemed because you've already admitted that it was exactly that.'

'Rachel...'

He tried to catch hold of one of the hands she had been waving in the air, making wild gesticulations that revealed with painful clarity the frantic state of her mind. But with a strength born of desperation she pulled herself free, her chest heaving as she struggled to control the panic welling up inside her.

'So what was she, Gabriel? What was she doing there? Tell me! What?' she demanded when he muttered something she couldn't catch. 'What did you say?'

'A form of protection!' he flung at her, with a glare

that in anyone else she would have described as defiant. 'A defence!'

'Protection?' Rachel echoed incredulously. 'I don't believe you. A defence against what? Who? Not me!'

A brusque, hard inclination of his head was his only response, drawing a shaken and disbelieving laugh from her.

'Oh, now I've heard everything! If you expected me to believe you, you should have come up with a better story than that...'

A sudden noise broke harshly into her tirade. The buzzer on the oven, she realised after a second's startled silence.

'That's your supper,' she said sharply, grateful for the diversion.

When he muttered an obscene suggestion as to what she could do with his meal, she simply ignored him and marched into the kitchen, pulling on oven gloves and taking the pie roughly from the oven. With no care at all, she hacked out a large piece and slammed it onto a waiting plate.

'Salad?' she snapped, knowing from the way that all the tiny hairs on her skin had lifted, acting as an early-warning device, that he had come up behind her.

'Rachel...' He sounded ominously close to the very end of his tether. 'How many times do I have to tell you that I don't want any bloody food?'

'Well, there's nothing else on offer! I don't fall into that sort of trap twice!'

'I should hope to hell there isn't!' He sounded so horrified that it was like a brutal slap in the face. 'There are only so many times that a man can say no to temptation!'

Rachel's hands clenched over the edge of the worktop until the knuckles showed white. It was what he had said that night in his room, she recalled, the taste of her misery sour in her mouth. He had used virtually the same words as he had joined her in his bed.

The memory of the consideration he had shown her

tore at her already desolated heart. She had let his concern for her pleasure deceive her, believing that it made her someone special in his eyes, someone he cared for.

Now she realised it had just been the action of an experienced man determined to prove his reputation as a lover. It had probably done his ego a power of good to know that he could bring even an untried virgin such as herself to orgasm on her very first night.

There was a question that had to be asked. With a controlled effort she forced her fingers to relax their grip and swung round to face him.

'Tell me something. If Amanda was "protection"...' She used the way she spat out the word to demonstrate just what she thought of that claim. 'Then what, pray, is poor Cassie? Why are you marrying her?'

'Because I have to,' was the stark, emotionless response.

'Because...?'

The impact of the full meaning of his words threatened to make her knees buckle. So she had been deceived even in this. The love match she had foolishly believed in had no existence outside her imagination. He was only prepared to marry because there was a baby on the way. So much for being the best husband he could!

Blind fury on Cassie's behalf blended with the pain she felt for herself to create a volatile mixture that was as devastating and explosive as any Molotov cocktail.

'You bastard!'

His supper plate was within easy reach. Before she had even consciously formed the thought, she had snatched it up and flung it straight at his face.

'You hateful, despicable, bastard!'

The easy way he dodged her makeshift missile was the last straw. Sidestepping neatly, he let the plate smash against the wall, sliding to the floor in a mess of shattered crockery, puff pastry and creamy chicken.

Unable to bear even being in the same room as him

any longer, Rachel gave a wild, choking cry and ran from the kitchen, blundering desperately across the hall and up the stairs.

'Rachel!'

He was coming after her, using the advantage of his longer legs to take the stairs two at a time, getting closer by the second. She didn't dare to look back, but concentrated on not missing her footing when trying to see through eyes so blurred with tears she might just as well have been blind.

'Rachel, wait…'

He caught her up at the door to her bedroom. Cruel fingers closed over her shoulders, bringing her to an abrupt halt. Hard arms clamped round her, holding her still in spite of her struggles.

'Let me go! Let me *go*, damn you!'

She aimed a savage kick at his ankles and had the satisfaction of hearing his muffled grunt of pain as her toe made contact with the bone. But the dark smile of triumph vanished from her face when his grip didn't so much as loosen. Instead he shouldered open the door, pulling her into the room with him.

'Rachel, sit down. *Sit down*!'

'I won't do anything you say! Nothing—do you hear?'

Something seemed to snap inside Rachel's mind. She felt such a rush of pain, of anger, such a devastating sense of betrayal that it overwhelmed her. She wanted to shout and scream, but no words would come.

Somehow she got her hands up inside the imprisoning grip of his arms, her self-control shattering completely as she pounded her fists against his chest. She lashed out wildly, as if only physical violence could appease the agony in her heart, aiming frantic blows at his shoulders, his arms, even his face.

And Gabriel did nothing to stop her. Apart from one swift, defensive jerk of his head out of reach of her hands, he just took it, waiting, silent and impassive, until the fury burned itself out.

Only then did he manoeuvre her onto the bed, sitting down beside her and hauling her up against him. Still he didn't say a word, just held her until the frantic pounding of her heart eased, the raging tide ebbed, and with a sobbing, shuddering cry she lay still and exhausted against his chest.

Only then did he draw in a deep, uneven breath, straightening his shoulders as if accepting some sort of burden that he knew he could not escape. Strong, square-tipped fingers slid under her chin, and when she resisted he simply exerted a little more pressure until she was forced to lift her face to his. It was impossible to avoid the dark, impenetrable depths of his eyes.

'First things first—no, listen to me!' he insisted when she tried, impotently, to twist away. 'I have never, ever slept with Cassie since I met her, and I never will until we are married.'

Shock held Rachel rigid as the words sank in, and at last she found her tongue again.

'Not until... But you said...!'

'I'm marrying her because I have to, yes, but not in the way you think. She isn't carrying my child, if that's what you believe.'

'Then why...?'

The dark eyes dropped, avoiding her searching gaze.

'Don't ask, Rachel. For God's sake, leave it there.'

But she couldn't. She couldn't leave it with so many questions still unanswered, with one vital problem uppermost in her thoughts.

'And me?' she asked shakily.

His hard, set face softened suddenly. After the tension of just moments before, the appalling sense of danger, the threat of terrible disaster, his sudden gentleness was almost shocking.

'You were—are—special, and always will be.'

'So special that within a couple of days you'd forgotten me, turned to someone else!'

'Oh, hell, Rachel, no! I never *forgot* you! I couldn't!'

Why did she believe him now? Why did the emphasis on those words ring true when it hadn't done so before? Because she *did* believe him, and the thought that perhaps she had meant more to him than he had ever admitted went some way to soothing the acid burn inside her heart.

'And now?'

'Rachel…'

It was a groan of despair, but threaded through it was an unmistakable edge of surrender, one that hadn't been there before. Focusing on that, Rachel sensed that the truth was near, if she only had the strength and determination to pursue it.

Tilting her head back so that it was resting on his shoulder, the hard strength of his arm supporting her back, she looked up into his face.

And this time he didn't try to avoid her eyes. This time he met her searching gaze head-on, with a sombre intensity that lifted the hair at the back of her neck on a shiver of apprehension.

But she couldn't go back. She couldn't stop now. She sensed intuitively that she was on the verge of something so important, so revelatory that it would change her life for ever. Whether the change would be for good or bad, she couldn't begin to guess. She only knew that if she ran from it now it would haunt her day and night.

'How do you think of me now?'

Gabriel swallowed hard. She saw the convulsive movement of the muscles in his throat and knew that she had read him right. He could no longer dodge the issue. He would tell her, but only if she pressed him. The decision was hers.

'Gabriel, I have to know! Do you have any feelings…?'

'Feelings!' It was a sound of pain. 'Oh, God, Rachel, if you only knew!'

'Then tell me! Do you want me...?'

'God help me, yes, I do!'

The declaration was rough-voiced, distinctly ragged at the edges, sounding as if it had been dragged from him with pliers. His fierce eyes never left hers, barely even blinked as he continued.

'Rachel, angel, I more than want you! I adore you. I love you with all my heart. If I could, I would marry you today—if you'd have me.'

'If I'd—'' Rachel began, but his hand came up swiftly to cover her mouth, cutting her off almost roughly.

'I can think of nothing I want more,' he went on in that raw, husky voice that sounded as if he had only just rediscovered the power of speech after a century of silence, 'than to live the rest of my life with you, have children with you, grow old by your side...'

As a declaration of love it was just about perfect. It should have lifted her heart, should have filled her mind with such an explosion of delight that she might swoon just to think of it. But there was a nasty little trickle of cold unease down her spine, contaminating the moment and taking all the joy from it.

'If I could', he had said.

Removing his hand from her mouth, she curled her own fingers round it so that he couldn't suppress any more questions.

'Then why don't you?'

For the first time since he had opened his heart to her his eyes fell away from hers, focusing blankly on a point somewhere on the carpet by his feet.

'Because I can't. I must not. *We* must not.'

'Can't! Must not!'

Rachel couldn't believe what she was hearing.

'Gabriel, those words don't come into it! I love you. You love me. I *love* you,' she repeated, when an involuntary sideways jerk of his head seemed to deny her ardent declaration. 'So what in the world is there to stop us from being together?'

He didn't answer her question; instead, he parried it with another, low-toned and lifeless, with no inflexion whatsoever.

'What is it you want from me, Rachel?'

'Want? Isn't it obvious? Do I have to spell it out? I want to go back five and a half years and root out whatever silly, invented moral objections you put in the way of our relationship then. Whether you thought I was too young, or too naive, I want you to forget you ever felt that way! I want to start again…'

His very stillness, the tension that held his long frame taut beside her, was stretching her nerves to breaking point, making them jangle in panic. She had to break through to him, jolt him out of the black trance that held him prisoner, turning his eyes opaque, leaching the blood from his skin.

Deliberately she moved closer, pressing up against his unresponsive body.

'Gabriel, what I really want is for you to kiss me stupid. And then I want you to pick me up, put me on this bed, strip me naked and make mad, passionate love to me until we're both too sated, too exhausted to think, and every last crazy, mistaken scruple is driven from your mind.'

He was tempted. He couldn't hide it. It showed in every inch of him, in his harsh, uneven breathing.

He was tempted, but fighting it, damn him! Fighting it hard. She could read the brutal battle in his eyes as she saw that burning black gaze go to her face, then to the bed and back.

'Oh, God!'

One hand, strangely cold, reached out to touch her cheek, the caress soft as the fall of a single snowflake, drawing an instinctive murmur of response from her parted lips.

'Oh, *God*!' he said, on a very different note.

The next moment his arms had closed around her, pulling her towards him with an urgency that bordered on roughness, telling her without any words that simple touch was not enough, not nearly enough.

He crushed a kiss onto her lips, a wild, fiercely overwhelming kiss that spoke of love and longing, of need and passion, and a terrible, hungry desperation.

Rachel responded with every bit as much passion as he had given her. She showed him exactly the same degree of need, of aching, burning longing.

Whatever roughly built barrier had held back their feelings for each other over the past five and a half years, it was finally breached, letting the floodwaters of desire pour past it, rushing, swirling, unable to be contained any longer. Sweeping aside everything in their path, they thundered towards the fulfilment that had been denied for too long.

But just as Rachel's heart began to soar like a caged wild bird suddenly finding itself free, just as it threatened to break free from her body and fly upwards, heading straight for the sun, just as her mouth softened under his, opening to invite the intimate invasion of his tongue that she craved so desperately, just as she began to melt against him, he wrenched himself free with a desperate cry that froze her blood in her veins just to hear it.

'No! Damn it to hell—*no*!'

His darkly eloquent stream of obscenities was a brutal testimony to the violence of his feelings. Hearing them, Rachel felt as if two cruel hands had gripped her heart, twisting it savagely.

Abruptly the vicious tirade ceased. Gabriel closed his eyes and was suddenly very still, totally, frighteningly immobile except for his hands, which had clenched into tight, unyielding fists as his breath hissed in between his clenched teeth.

Three terrified heartbeats later, the tight-fastened lids opened slowly again to reveal the marble opacity she had come to dread. With a gentleness that was strangely shocking in contrast to all that had gone before, he cupped her cheek in one hand before touching his mouth to hers for one tender, heartbreakingly brief moment.

His breath was warm against her skin for a second, and she could have sworn that his lips silently formed the word 'goodbye'. Then, gently but firmly, with a finality that allowed for no appeal, he put her away from him and stood up.

He had no need to do anything more to drive home his message. But, obviously needing to make it absolutely clear, he underlined his mental distance from her with a physical one, moving to put the entire length of the room between them.

'*Gabriel*!' Her voice came and went erratically, all control lost. 'What is it? Why…?'

'I *can't*!'

'But *why*? Is it because you still think of me as being too young? I'm not your little sister any more.'

She would have sworn that it was impossible for him to lose any more colour, but she saw his skin turn ashen, shocking against the terrible darkness of his eyes.

'That's exactly the problem, sweetheart.' In contrast to the look on his face, his voice had found a new strength from somewhere, though it was rusty and as uneven as her own had been.

'The little sister thing?'

Relief was like a rush of adrenalin to her head, making it swim in delight so that she laughed out loud.

'Not that old nonsense! *Gabriel*! Not any longer! You know I…'

The words died as she saw the change in his expression. Blazing torment flared in his eyes, driving away the coldly carved look and turning his face into a harrowed mask, a death's head with molten sockets.

'Not that sort of sister,' he choked out. 'A real sister—of the same blood! Rachel, my love, we're intimately related. My father was your father too. It would be obscene. That night was—it would have been…'

Even he couldn't form the word. And as her horror-stricken mind supplied those two damning syllables Rachel felt those brutal hands clench viciously on her heart again, inflicting such agony that she thought she might actually die from the pain.

'It can't be! I won't believe it!'

'Believe it! *Please* believe it!' His desperation convinced where nothing else could. 'Believe it and forget any dreams you might have had of the two of us having any sort of future together. Forget them for ever, and find someone else.'

'No—never!'

Hearing her agonised vehemence, he made a move to come to her side. But then immediately he reconsidered, forcing himself into stillness with an effort that rammed home the dreadful reality of what he had said more than any words could ever do.

'You must, Rachel,' he said, with a softness that tore at her heart. 'It's the only way; there's no alternative. You have to do it. As I...'

Of course. Cassie.

'As you have.'

His slow nod was the final admission of total, hopeless defeat.

'As I have. Now do you see why I have to marry Cassie? If I can't have you then I can never truly love anyone. But I'll keep my vows to her, be the best husband I can ever be to anyone who isn't you. That's my only hope of salvation.'

CHAPTER ELEVEN

RACHEL stared sightlessly at her drawing board, a pencil dangling limply from the lifeless fingers of her right hand. For four days now she had tried to keep up a pretence of working, or at least functioning, but she doubted she was convincing anyone, least of all herself.

Outwardly she might look in control. She got dressed, put on make-up, went to work. She moved, she talked, she even forced coffee down a throat that seemed to have shrunk to the size of a pinhead from being so permanently constricted. She didn't eat; eating was beyond her.

But inwardly she was falling apart. Inside she knew she was barely holding together with the use of sticking plaster and bits of string. Her heart was just one raw, bloody mess. Every now and then another bit would tear off from it if she so much as let her thoughts drift towards the events of the previous Friday night.

She *looked* all right. Pale, perhaps, in a way that even the most careful make-up couldn't disguise, and with eyes red-rimmed from lack of sleep. But no worse than anyone else who might have spent the weekend in bed with the violent stomach bug that she had used as an excuse to cover any change in her appearance or demeanour.

But this time her eyes weren't swollen and raw, as they had been five and a half years before, this time she was denied even the release of the tears that at nineteen had flooded down her cheeks, soaking into her pillow and reducing her to an abject, exhausted bundle of misery. This time there was no way of letting out the anguish, the horror, the sheer, soul-destroying agony of what had happened.

If it was possible, Gabriel looked worse than she did. She only knew that because she had met him on the doorstep on the one occasion when his ruthlessly determined campaign of arranging his arrival at or departure from the house had gone badly wrong. Normally he planned it like a military manoeuvre, ensuring that he was only ever in the house if she was at work. If she was at home then he was out. At Cassie's, presumably.

The arrangements for the wedding were still going ahead with a dreadful, unstoppable inevitability. But anyone with eyes to see must realise that the groom's heart wasn't in it. Or perhaps he put on a far better act for them than he had been able to show to her.

'Oh, Gabriel...'

Sighing deeply, Rachel pushed a hand through hair that was dishevelled and tangled by too many repetitions of the same despondent action. Once more she tried to force herself to focus on the design in front of her, only to find her eyes brimming with stinging tears as the sound of Gabriel's voice saying, 'I want you to design something very special for me,' echoed inside her head.

If only she had simply agreed to his request. If only she hadn't pushed to know why he was marrying Cassie. If only she had never been told the truth!

Or would living in blind ignorance be any better? Would it hurt any less to have Gabriel adamantly refuse to have anything to do with her and not know why? He had fought so hard against telling her, but she had insisted on an answer.

Well, now she knew. And the truth she had been so determined on had taken her world, smashed it against a hard, unyielding wall of horror, and shattered it into a million tiny irreparable splinters.

She hadn't believed him, of course. She had refused to accept what he had told her. Even with that appalling admission still hanging in the air between them she had tried to find some way out of the nightmare into which she had fallen headlong.

'How did you find out all this?' she had asked, once she had finally recovered enough strength to speak. 'Where did you get this dreadful story from?'

'Your mother,' Gabriel returned flatly.

'My *mother* said—and you believed her?'

From the total darkness of despair she suddenly thought she had moved to a point where she saw a tiny speck of light.

'You know how much she hated you in those days. She would have said anything to keep us apart. And yet you swallowed—'

'Not just what she said!' Gabriel inserted roughly. 'I asked my father too.'

Slowly he shook his dark head, eyes black with despair as he looked back through time, seeming to be present once more at that dreadful confrontation.

'After that night...'

There was no need to spell it out. They both knew exactly which night he meant.

'I knew then that I loved you. That I wanted more than just a casual affair. But I also knew that your mama would do everything she could to put barriers in our way, especially as you were so young. So I decided to talk to her, tell her I had—feelings for you.'

Rachel's head came up swiftly, grey eyes dark with panic.

'You didn't...?'

'No, love.'

The soft, soothing tone, the way the endearment had slipped past his guard, tore at her heart.

'I didn't tell her what had happened. Only that over the past six months I...' His laughter was brittle, cruelly self-deprecatory. 'I hadn't been able to see you as my adopted sister any longer. So would she mind if I took you out once or twice.'

This time the amusement was even darker, making Rachel want to turn away and bury her head in the pillow, anything other than have to hear what he was going to say. Gabriel paced over to the huge window on the opposite wall and stared broodingly out at the gathering dusk.

'Her reply was blunt and very much to the point. I dated you only if I wanted to risk scandal, shame and a possible prison sentence. It was high time I knew the facts, and the truth was that her affair with my father hadn't started in the year before he moved the two of you into this house. In fact they had been lovers on and off for nearly twenty years.'

Gabriel paused to let the ominous significance of that fact sink in. But Rachel needed no such thinking time. She could remember how, when she'd been thirteen, her mother had introduced her to 'Uncle Greg' with the explanation that 'He and I used to be friends a long time ago'. And Gabriel himself had told her how his father—*her* father too!—had described her playing with modelling clay as a small child.

'So my...' Hastily she caught up the inaccurate word 'dad'. 'John Amis—my mother's husband...'

'Was someone who couldn't have children of his own,' Gabriel continued. 'He met Lydia after one of her periodic bust-ups with my father. Apparently she was already pregnant with you, but Greg refused to acknowledge paternity. Amis married Lydia very quickly and registered the baby—you—as his own biological daughter. Your mother believed she'd never see Greg again so she didn't contradict the story, just let you grow up believing Amis was your father. Rachel, stop it!'

'Stop what?'

She stared at him blankly, only realising when a curt, silent nod directed her attention to it how she had pulled a handful of tissues from the box beside the bed and was systematically shredding them with fingers that were white with tension.

With a struggle she forced her hands tight shut. The fact that he had only told her to stop, making no move to come to her and still the nervous action himself, told its own painful story.

'You checked all this with your father?'

Another brief inclination of his dark head signified agreement.

'He admitted it had all happened exactly as Lydia had said. That they'd had an affair which had resulted in you being conceived, then they'd split up and your mother had married Amis, who died when you were just a kid. Greg and Lydia met up again some years later and their relationship took up where it had left off. Secretly, at first, but then when my mother moved out Greg brought you and Lydia here.'

'So when did she tell Greg...?'

'That you were his? Not at first. Lydia knew that if she told my father straight away that he'd simply see it as a money-grabbing stunt—that she was out to get an inheritance for you or trying to force his hand into marriage to her. Instead she waited, let Greg come to care for you.'

Gabriel sighed, pushing both hands roughly through his hair before swinging round to face her again.

'And he did care for you, darling... Oh, God!'

The speed, the obvious distaste with which he caught himself up slashed a brutal knife into Rachel's already agonised heart. Unable to hold back, needing desperately to comfort him, she was halfway to her feet when a furious glare from those burning dark eyes froze the movement.

The savage command, '*Don't*! Don't even think of it!' had her sinking back onto the bed with a sob of despair.

He was right, of course. She knew it, even if she couldn't bear to acknowledge it openly.

If they breached the barriers that Gabriel had fought so hard to erect between them, the consequences would be totally destructive of what little remained of their peace of mind. The thought that those barriers would have to stay in place for the rest of their lives was more than she could bear.

'He came to love you, Rachel,' Gabriel amended painfully. 'As I did. By the time he had the blood test that Lydia insisted on, the proof that you were his had ceased to matter.'

To Greg, perhaps, Rachel thought miserably. But to Gabriel it had mattered so very much. The results of that test had devastated his life, and now they were destroying hers.

'But why didn't my mother ever tell me this?'

'Greg forbade her to. He said he didn't want people knowing his business. I think he made it a condition of her coming to live here, and she wanted him so much that she stuck strictly to it, even after his death.'

'Then why didn't he want to acknowledge me?' she managed to ask.

Gabriel shook his head despairingly.

'God knows. If only he had, then we wouldn't have fallen into this cesspit of filth that's trapped us now. And of course we'll never know what he might have done after he married your mother. If he hadn't died then perhaps he'd have swallowed whatever stupid pride held him back and made us all one big happy family.'

The black cynicism of that last comment made Rachel wince away inside.

'This is what you quarrelled about, isn't it?'

Gabriel's nod of agreement was grim-faced, his mouth drawn into a hard, narrow line.

'He said it didn't matter whose child you were. You were here, treated as his daughter to all intents and purposes. What did anything else count for? I told him he should claim you, or at least marry Lydia, make it all legal. I wanted it all out in the open. I wanted you to have your rightful place, your rightful name, your real father…'

Once more he shook his head, as if in disbelief at his own thoughts.

'I wasn't thinking straight. You were only nineteen and I'd just taken your virginity...'

'Not *taken*!' Rachel had to insist. 'You took nothing I didn't want to give. I was as...'

The way a muscle moved convulsively as his jaw clenched and the white lines etched into his face told her she had missed the point.

'Oh...!'

'Yes.'

His tone harshly underlined the terrible impact of the realisation.

'If your paternity had become public, then you would have known that I was your half-brother. I didn't think you could handle it. Hell, *I* couldn't handle it! So I agreed with my father that things were better left unsaid, and I took myself off to America as fast as I could.'

'Having first made sure that I would never, ever want to come near you again,' Rachel put in, full understanding of just what he had done thickening her voice with tears.

'Yes.' It was a thin thread of sound, barely audible. 'You'll never know how much that cost me. But I couldn't see any other way out. I couldn't tell you the truth, and I couldn't risk you coming on to me again.'

His smile was wry, heartbreakingly lopsided, and so obviously in contrast to the thoughts in his head that she wanted to cry out, beg him to stop.

'I didn't think I'd be able to resist you. And I knew I'd have to say no, that I wouldn't be able to do it gently. I was terrified that my reaction would give something away. I know I hurt you, but it was better than having you find out the truth.'

And he had been prepared to have her hate him. He had loved her enough to bear her scorn, her disgust, her contempt all these years in order to protect her from the consequences of her own actions.

'And Amanda was just a defence?'

Gabriel's short bark of laughter was bleaker than before, and cold enough to splinter the air.

'Only just. She got very little satisfaction from that night. I'm only surprised she didn't spread the truth around then, or after I'd gone: Gabriel Tiernan, reputed stud of this parish, unable to perform! I *meant* to. I really believed I could lose myself in her, blot out all thought of you, find the oblivion I needed. But when it came down to it—nothing!'

Was it wrong to feel not just relief but a surge of happiness at his declaration? If it was, then Rachel couldn't admit to any guilt at the thought. She wouldn't have been human, or genuinely in love, if she hadn't been glad that Amanda hadn't taken her place so easily.

'And Cassie?'

'Cassie?'

Gabriel's hands smoothed over his face, palms rubbing against his eyes in a gesture of exhausted defeat.

'Cassie is the shield you forced me to use against you.'

'*I* did?' Rachel protested disbelievingly, and Gabriel nodded solemnly.

'When I came back here for my father's funeral, I believed—I prayed—that the four and a half years I'd been away had been long enough. That when I met you again I would have got over my feelings for you, or at least grown a thicker skin so that I would be able to keep them well under control for as long as it took to sort things out here and hightail it back to the States. I was wrong.'

With a deep sigh he slumped back against the wall, as if he no longer had the mental strength to keep himself upright.

'God, was I wrong! As soon as I set eyes on you I knew that nothing had died. It hadn't even *weakened*; if anything it was stronger. You were no longer a girl, but a fully grown woman, more beautiful than ever before. It was all still there, just below the surface, waiting to spring back into life again. I told myself I could handle it—I had to handle it. I *would* have handled it if you'd stayed angry. If you'd kept on hating me, kept your distance…'

'But I couldn't,' Rachel said softly, and saw his head move in despondent acknowledgement of a force that was greater than either of them.

'You couldn't, and neither could I. I had only to look at you to want you. Touch you and I'd go up in flames. Three days, that was all it took before I found myself running back to America, terrified of the way I'd come so close to blowing the lid off a very nasty can of worms indeed. I knew then that I'd have to do something else, something more definite—something final.'

'I certainly never planned on coming back here until I was married.' Now, when she was quite unable to bear it, Gabriel's declaration on the night before his father's—*their* father's—funeral came back to haunt her.

'I would never have dared to face you again on my own.'

Once more that heartfelt sigh seemed to have been dragged up right from the depths of his soul.

'I'm very fond of Cassie, Rachel. I can never love her in the way I love you, but I think I can make her happy. I'll try my bloody best to do so; she deserves that consideration. If I could have married her quietly and quickly in America, I would have preferred that. But Cass wanted the full works, and it had to be here, in London, nowhere else. When it's over we'll go back to New York to stay. You need never see—'

'*No*!' It was more than she could bear. 'Gabriel, no—please!'

'Yes.'

The single syllable was coldly inimical, as hard and unyielding as the set of his jaw, the ice in his eyes.

'That's the way it has to be, Rachel. I can't settle for a lifetime of loving you as just a sister. I've tried, and it tore me apart. When Cassie and I are married, I'm leaving for good. And if you're wise you'll forget all about me, find someone else.'

'Never! I couldn't!'

Her defiant answer broke the icy calm he had built around his feelings. Stunned and horrified, she watched his control crumble, his eyes blaze with pain.

'Oh, God, sweetheart, don't say that! You have to find someone—rebuild your life. If I could think of you being somewhere in the world, and happy, then I think I could cope.'

Happy? Without him? It was impossible. But she knew that to say so would only add immeasurably to what he was already feeling, and so she bit down hard on her tongue, forcing herself to remain silent.

Slowly, wearily, like a man who had aged ten years in the time he had been talking, Gabriel levered himself away from the wall.

'And now I'm going.'

'To Cassie.'

Pain tore it from her lips. Pain that intensified to an unbearable pitch when he nodded slowly.

'To Cassie,' he confirmed with sombre finality. 'It's either that or get so blindly, stinkingly out of my head that I can no longer even *think*. But if I did get drunk I couldn't trust myself not to come back here, and I'm not doing that. Not until your mother's here to act as chaperon again. If I could, I'd move somewhere else until the wedding, but that would only start people asking questions we don't want them to know the answers to.'

'Gabriel...' Rachel tried to protest, but he held up a hand to silence her.

'Rachel, please, let me do this. Don't make things any harder than they are already. We have no choice; you know that.'

But how could she let him go, knowing it was for ever? That they would never be alone together again?

'Couldn't you just kiss me goodbye? Just one kiss?'

She knew the answer even as she spoke, but still the

slow, adamant shake of his head was the hardest thing she had ever had to endure.

'You know I can't, angel. Because it wouldn't be just one kiss. If I touch you again, I won't be answerable for the consequences. So let me go, sweetheart; it's the only thing I can do for you. Let me go, but always remember that no matter where I am or what I'm doing you will always be with me in my heart and in my thoughts, and no one can ever take that away.'

She didn't know how she found the strength to let it happen. How she managed to sit still and watch him walk towards the door.

Somehow she coped with the moment when, at the last minute, he turned and their eyes met, dark chocolate locking with smoky grey for a long, poignant moment. She even forced a weak, wan smile so that he could remember it for ever afterwards. The silvery trails of tears on her pale cheeks she could do nothing about.

'I love you,' were the last words he said, and they shimmered in the air through a haze of tears as he finally walked away, the door swinging to silently behind him.

Rachel held out while she could hear his slow, heavy footsteps descending the stairs. She kept herself ruthlessly under control until they reached the hallway and faded away.

It was only when she heard the front door slam, the roar of his car's engine in the still of the night, that the brutal hands that had tormented her earlier renewed their assault on her heart. This time they completed their monstrous task as they slowly, irrevocably tore it in two.

'Rachel! *Rachel!* Hey, dreamer—phone!'

'What?'

Blinking in shocked confusion, Rachel stared round at where, through the open door, her secretary was waving her telephone receiver in the air.

'Phone!' she said again. 'For you!'

'Oh—coming!'

But before she could get to her feet, desperately trying to gather the shattered remnants of her composure around her, Alice had put the instrument to her ear again.

'What? But... All right, then, I'll tell her. They've gone,' she said as Rachel finally reached her.

'Gone? But who was it?'

'She didn't give a name. But she said she had a message from your mother.'

'Mum?'

Now Rachel was really confused. Why would her mother ask someone else to phone her? Unless...

'Is there a problem? Something wrong?'

'Not with your mum, but she said that Gabriel—is that *the* Gabriel? Mr Tiernan?'

'Gabriel!' All Rachel's senses were on red alert. 'What about Gabriel?'

'He's not well, she said. It seems there's some problem with his heart.'

His *heart*! Already she was hurrying back to her desk, snatching up her handbag and pulling on the jacket of her smart dark green suit.

'Where did they say I should go?'

'To the house. You'd better hurry. She said it was important...' The words became inaudible as Rachel ran from the room.

Gabriel not well. A problem with his heart. Oh, God, please, please let him be all right! Please!

The word was a litany of panic on her lips as she turned her Escort out of the car park, putting her foot down as soon as the road was clear.

'Please! Please!'

Luckily the traffic was only light, the damp, typically English spring day keeping the usual hordes of playing schoolchildren inside for a change. Rachel's attention wasn't fully on her driving, instead already leaping ahead to what she might find at the Richmond house.

His heart? He was too young, too fit to have a heart

attack surely? Or could it be some congenital weakness? Or…

Oh, God, no! Her blood iced as an appalling thought pushed its way, unwanted, into her mind.

He *wouldn't*, couldn't think of anything so dreadful as suicide, could he? He had looked terrible when she had last seen him, but was he *that* low, that depressed?

At last she reached the house, slamming on the brakes with no regard for the engine or where she was parked. Leaping out of the car, she dashed in through the already open front door.

'Gabriel!' Her voice echoed round the empty hallway. 'Oh, God, *Gabriel*! Where are you?'

There was no response, no sound from any part of the house. He must be in his room. In bed perhaps. She was halfway up the staircase when she heard the sound of a second car, driven even more wildly than her own, pulling up outside in a spray of gravel.

'Rachel! For God's sake, Rachel, where are you?'

It was an uncanny echo of her own arrival, but the voice she heard stopped her dead, freezing with her foot half-raised to take the next step.

It couldn't be! Slowly she turned to see the man who had just dashed into the hall. His hair was wildly dishevelled, his face a mask of fear and concern that she knew must mirror her own.

'Gabriel…'

'Rachel. Oh, thank God!'

Their voices clashed in a fervent declaration of relief.

'Gabriel, you're all right.'

She couldn't stop herself. No thought of resistance or propriety even entered her head. No force on earth could have stopped her in her headlong rush down the stairs again, leaping the last three in one as she flew straight into his waiting arms.

'You're really all right!' she gasped again when he finally loosened his convulsive hug enough to let her gather breath to speak.

'All right?' Gabriel's voice was shaken, as bewildered as her own. 'Of course I'm all right. It was you who was ill.'

'No.' Rachel shook her head emphatically. 'It was *you*. I got a phone call. Someone ringing on Mum's behalf. She said you were ill—hurt—something to do with...'

'With your heart,' Gabriel finished for her when her voice gave out as a result of the stress and confusion. 'That's the message they left for me too, but about you. But if you didn't send it...'

'I didn't! I never...'

'Then who the hell did?'

'I did.'

It was a new voice entirely. Soft but firm, it came from behind them, its owner concealed by the door into the sitting room which had been partially open all this time. As Rachel's head swung in that direction, silver eyes wide and hazed in shock, a female figure moved into the hall.

Tall, slender and elegant in a simple green dress, Cassie Elliot looked pale and strained but as lovely as ever, her big brown eyes very bright, her long, dark hair lying loose and tumbled on her shoulders.

'Cass!' Gabriel's voice was raw and husky, an anxious questioning note threading through the sound of her name. 'What...?'

He would have moved forward, taken her hand, but Cassie stopped him with a single graceful gesture.

'I sent those messages, Gabriel—both of them. I'm sorry if I worried you, but I had to know. I had to see if what I suspected was the truth.'

'What you suspected...' Gabriel echoed hoarsely, but it was a statement, not a question. He knew exactly what she meant, Rachel acknowledged, just as she had done when she had realised that the excessive brightness of the other woman's eyes was caused by the shimmer of unshed tears.

'I knew that if I asked, you wouldn't tell me.' Her smile was lopsided and sadly resigned. 'You've been trying to keep it from me all these weeks, but I've known something was up. I could see that you weren't happy, that you've been putting on a good pretence at being interested in the wedding, the prospect of our life together, but your heart isn't in it. I knew there was someone else.'

'Cassie…' Rachel tried, when Gabriel couldn't speak, but the other girl stilled her with another of those gentle smiles.

'Did you know he never stops talking about you? It's Rachel this and Rachel that. Rachel's designs, Rachel's clothes, Rachel's hair.'

'I'm sure he doesn't mean…' Rachel tried again.

'*I'm* sure he does!' Cassie corrected with a touch of bittersweet laughter. 'Love you, I mean. But he's so much of a dear fool that he hasn't actually realised what's happened to him. What is it, Gabriel?'

Her brown eyes went to his dark, shuttered face.

'Is it because you lived together when you were younger that you just can't see what's right under your nose?'

'Cassie—no!'

Gabriel's horrified exclamation seared over Rachel's exposed nerves, scraping away another layer of skin, leaving her whole body painfully sensitised. Beside her, Gabriel himself looked dreadful, his face as drawn and strained as if he was physically ill. Alone of the three of them, Cassie remained supremely calm.

'Yes, Gabriel,' she insisted gently. 'I'm no fool. I've known all along that you didn't love me the way I love you. I suspected from the start that there was someone else, but I thought she'd broken your heart because she didn't return your love. Then, when I met Rachel and saw you together, I knew she was the one.'

The brown eyes went to Rachel's face, Cassie even

managing a smile of empathy that twisted in Rachel's conscience.

'But what I couldn't understand was that it was so obvious she loved you too. You do, don't you?'

She directed the question at Rachel, who could find no answer but complete honesty.

'Yes, but—'

But Cassie wouldn't let her finish.

'And, knowing that, I could never come between you. All I could think of was that it had to be some silly fight or blind, foolish pride that was keeping you apart. So I concocted a little test. I sent those messages, and then I came here and waited. Mrs Reynolds let me in. If I'd had any doubts at all, they were wiped away as soon as I saw your faces. You more than love each other. You're soul mates.'

Drawing in a deep, deep breath, Cassie moved at last, walking towards Gabriel, tugging the ring from her left hand as she did so.

'I can't marry you, Gabriel. Not when I know I can never make you happy. It's better this way,' she added hurriedly, lifting a finger to silence him when he tried to protest. 'Believe me, you know it is.'

It was when Gabriel silently held out his hand that Rachel knew he had accepted what his fiancée had said. All the fight, all the life seemed to have gone out of him, and his burning eyes were the only sign of response in his dead face. When Cassie placed the diamond solitaire in his palm he dropped his dark gaze to stare down at where it lay like a bright, sparkling teardrop.

'I would have tried to make you happy,' he said at last, his voice rusty and uneven.

'I know,' she sighed. 'The problem is that "tried".'

Leaning forward, she pressed a brief, soft kiss on his lean cheek, then lifted her head to look straight into Rachel's cloudy eyes.

'Look after him,' she said softly. 'Promise me.'

Rachel tried twice to answer. Each time she opened

her mouth, but no words could force themselves past the knot of emotion that had closed her throat.

'And you, Gabriel,' Cassie went on. 'Look at things more clearly. See what's there, and take it. After all, Rachel isn't really your "little sister", as you call her. She never was related to you, and she's all grown-up now. She loves you. You love her. Be happy!'

Rachel didn't see her go. Her eyes were fixed on the man before her, on his blank, opaque gaze, the colourless cheeks, the tight line of his mouth. And when at last he moved, to clench his hand over the ring in his hand and fling it away from him, the controlled silence with which he reacted was a hundred times more shocking than the most violent stream of curses, or a savage anger.

Reacting on pure instinct, she reached out a hand to him, but before she could touch his arm he moved, jerking away from her, repulsing the gesture of sympathy as if her fingertips were made of molten steel.

'No!' His voice was low, desperate, the sound of a wild animal trapped and facing the hunter's blade. 'Don't touch me ever again! In fact, Rachel, if you're wise you'll go—get out now—and not come back until I've gone.'

'Gone?'

She had known it was inevitable. But still it tore at her agonisingly, ripping into a heart that she hadn't believed could sustain any more wounds.

'Where are you going?'

'New York—California—to hell! Anywhere that's far enough from here so that we never meet again.'

She wanted to cry out, wanted to wrap her arms around herself to stop herself from falling apart, to ease the anguish she knew he felt. She wanted to beg him not to go, not to leave her alone.

But she knew that to do so would be the cruellest action she had ever taken. She had looked into Gabriel's face and seen how close he was to the edge.

Cassie had been his shield. Now she was gone, and

with her his only defence against his feelings. He couldn't stay. They could never take the risk of being alone together again.

But he had done it three times already. Once when she had been nineteen, once after his father's funeral, and again just four days before. She didn't have to be told to know that he couldn't do it again. This time she had to be the one to take the initiative.

And so, without another word, she turned and walked away from him. Walked out towards the bleakest, darkest, most desolate future she could imagine. And as she went through the door into the damp, miserable day, the rain began to fall more heavily, mingling with the tears on her cheeks so that even she could not have said which were which.

CHAPTER TWELVE

THE ring of the doorbell was the very last sound that Rachel wanted to hear.

She had just got home from an absolutely impossible day at work. A day spent pretending to be busy, pretending to listen if someone spoke, pretending to be interested in what everyone else was doing, when all the time she was dying inside. She had finally given up and, pleading a sick headache, fled for the sanctuary of her home.

The headache had become a painful reality by the time she reached the house, making her grateful for the fact that her mother was out. Judging by the silence from Gabriel's room, he had gone out too. Either that, or he was deliberately not responding to her call.

It was most likely the former, she'd decided miserably. After the traumatic events of the day before, he had returned strictly to his policy of being out when she was in, and she knew that was how it would be until he finally returned to America once and for all. He had already booked a flight, but hadn't said anything about exactly when he would be leaving.

She had settled herself on the settee with a mug of tea and a couple of painkillers when the bell sounded. Groaning aloud, she resolved to ignore it. Company in any form was the last thing she needed.

But she had reckoned without Mrs Reynolds, who had hurried to answer the summons. Hearing her tell the visitor that 'Miss Amis is in, if you'd like to step inside,' Rachel resigned herself to having her peace destroyed.

'Mrs Tiernan!' the housekeeper announced a moment later.

Mrs Tiernan? For a couple of confused seconds Rachel wondered just why her mother would ring at her own door, or want to be announced in this way.

But then realisation dawned with a jolt to her system, and when she saw the woman Mrs Reynolds ushered into the room she knew there was only one person she could be.

The dark hair, the wide-set deep brown eyes, the elegant height, and patrician features could only belong to the *first* Mrs Tiernan. Gabriel's mother. Gabriel had said that she was coming to England for the wedding, but surely she wasn't expected for another week?

The older woman's smile was warm, touched with apology.

'I hope you don't mind. I've come to see Gabriel.'

Even the name had the power to hurt. Would the agony ever ease? Perhaps in time it would settle down to just a bruised ache. She couldn't believe it would ever really go away.

'I'm afraid he's not here at the moment.'

'Of course, I should have realised. He'll be with Cassie. I know I said I'd fly over next week, but I decided on impulse to spend an extra week with my son. I was lucky enough to get a cancellation—I didn't even have time to ring him and let him know. I should have done that first; I'm sorry.'

'Not at all,' Rachel put in hastily. 'But, to be honest, I don't think he'll be with Cassie. I mean—oh, dear, it's obvious you haven't heard.'

She'd been in the air for close to twenty-four hours. Even if Gabriel had phoned to let her know of recent events, he would have missed her.

'Not heard what?' Gabriel's mother frowned her confusion. 'Is there a problem?'

'You could say that.' Rachel's voice cracked on the words. 'But I'm not sure it's my place to tell you.'

'Place or not, you're going to have to say something now. You've got me intrigued and I won't leave until I find out what's been going on.'

When she smiled like that, all charm but with a core of steel underneath that warned against any attempt to dodge the issue, she was Gabriel through and through. To her dismay, Rachel found herself blinking back tears as she struggled for the composure she needed.

'In that case, you'd better sit down.'

'Oh, dear, that sounds rather ominous. Is it that bad?'

Rachel could only nod, the tears she had forced down choking any attempt at speech. Lily Tiernan's smile faded and she leaned forward to take the younger woman's hand.

'I really think you'd better tell me. Is it about the wedding?'

'There isn't going to be one,' Rachel declared starkly, past thinking of a way to cushion the hard fact. 'Gabriel and Cassie—they've broken off the engagement. Well, Cassie has. Because—because...'

'Because of you,' Lily put in with an astute perception that astounded her. 'You *are* Rachel, aren't you?'

'Yes, but...'

'Oh, thank God!' Gabriel's mother declared fervently, stunning her even more. 'At last that silly boy has seen sense.'

'Sense?' Rachel could only echo shakenly, disturbed almost as much by hearing Gabriel described as a silly boy as by Lily's heartfelt exclamation.

Lily Tiernan nodded firmly.

'He's loved you for years. Always has done, almost from the moment he first set eyes on you. He used to say that he was just waiting for you to grow up.'

Her smile was softer, with a warmth that stabbed straight at Rachel's heart with the memory of the times, so rare but so precious, when Gabriel had looked at her in just that way.

'But then, about five years ago, he changed. He said there was no future with you, that he'd made a big mistake. Personally, I never believed it. I mean, for a long time he showed no interest in any woman. But then the next thing I knew he announced he was marrying this Cassie. I could only assume that you had never returned his feelings—'

She broke off sharply at the sight of the tears that could no longer be held back but were pouring down Rachel's colourless cheeks.

'Oh, my dear, what is it? *Do* you love him?'

'With all my heart.'

Rachel swiped at the tears with the back of her hand, but as fast as she brushed them aside others took their place. Having hidden her misery until now, she found that once the barriers were breached she could no longer hold back.

'But it's all ruined. I love him but I can never marry him. It would be wrong. And Gabriel...'

She couldn't go any further. Breaking down completely, she wept her heart out. Raw, racking sobs that came from deep inside, torn from her by the pain she could no longer endure.

Through a blur of tears she was aware of Lily moving to her side, putting her arms round her, simply holding her until the storm had passed. Then, reaching into her handbag, she pulled out a pristine handkerchief which she pressed into Rachel's limp fingers.

'I think you and I had better talk—and I mean *really* talk. Now, blow your nose and tell me just who put these crazy ideas into your head.'

'Gabriel!' Rachel gasped painfully. 'And they're not ideas, but facts. Horrible, hateful facts!'

It all came pouring out now, every last, dreadful detail of what Gabriel had confessed to her. It came out without pause, without hesitation, even when she came to the worst admission of all: the fact that she was Greg Tiernan's illegitimate daughter. And all the time Lily Tiernan listened with an unexpected calm, not saying anything except for the occasional murmur of encouragement that helped her to go on.

When the whole sorry tale was finished, and Rachel had subsided into desolate silence, Lily drew in a deep, slow breath and expelled it in a sigh. Getting to her feet, she crossed the room to press the bell that would summon Mrs Reynolds.

'What we both need is a stiff tea,' she said, and for all her outward calm there was a catch in her voice that told Rachel she wasn't unaffected by all she had heard. 'And then, when you're calm enough to listen, I'll tell you something about my son. Something I've never breathed a word of to anyone in my whole life.'

Long after Lily had left, Rachel sat curled up in her chair, staring into space, trying to get her head round everything she had just heard. It was all so amazing that she hadn't fully absorbed any of it, least of all its effect on her own future. She was so lost in thought that she didn't hear the car pull up outside, only becoming aware of Gabriel's presence in the house when he spoke to her from the doorway.

'Rachel?' Her name was a sound of concern. 'What are you doing home at this time of day?'

Her head jerked up sharply, misty grey eyes meeting shadowed brown. He looked exhausted, she thought sadly. Dressed all in black that accentuated his pallor, he appeared worn down with a weariness that was more than just a bone-deep physical sensation.

What she had to tell him could change all that, but she couldn't just blurt it out. She had barely registered it herself.

'Just thinking,' she said carefully. 'Where have you been?'

'Out.'

When he saw that his curt, evasive answer wouldn't satisfy her, he added almost grudgingly, 'I walked beside the river for a long time, trying to get my head together. And I went to see Cassie. I had to talk to her, apologise properly for hurting her the way I did.'

'Is she all right?' Concern for the other girl rang in Rachel's voice. She had had enough experience of unhappiness herself to empathise with what Cassie might be going through.

'She's coping. I think she knew our marriage would never have worked, never have made her happy. Deep down we both felt we weren't right for each other, and she had the courage to stop it before things went too far.'

'She's a lovely person,' Rachel said, meaning it completely. 'She deserves to be happy. In some ways she's very like your mother.'

'My mother?'

Something flared in his eyes. Concern? Apprehension? She couldn't read the emotion clearly.

'When did you see my mother?'

'She was here this afternoon. She flew over early on an impulse and came here looking for you. We had a long talk.'

'About what?'

He was definitely wary now, moving into the room to stand uneasily, like some wild animal poised ready for flight if she made the wrong move.

'About you, mostly. And a bit about her relationship with Greg too. She left you a letter.'

Gabriel's doubt and confusion showed in the frown that drew his dark brows together.

'A letter? But why?'

It was a struggle to remain calm and controlled when

she wanted to leap out of the chair, push the letter into his hands and beg him to read it. If she could hold back from telling him the whole story herself first.

But she had to take things carefully. She was not sure how much more he could cope with, even if it was good news. His face was drawn, and his control had a worryingly brittle quality about it, as if at any moment it might splinter completely.

'You'd better read it and see.'

Uncurling her legs from underneath her, she got slowly to her feet, holding out the white envelope that she had been holding in her lap.

Lily had suggested this approach as the best way to get the truth across. Gabriel had lived with a lot of inaccurate facts and false assumptions for most of his life. It would be difficult to take in the truth all at once. A letter would give it to him more gradually. It would seem like more solid, definite evidence.

Rachel had agreed at the time. But right now her nerves were stretched tight with the tension of wanting to follow Lily's advice and yet needing to have Gabriel know the truth as quickly as possible. She felt she might actually scream if he continued to stare at the letter as if he didn't recognise what it was.

'Take it!' she said, her inner sense of urgency making the command sharp and rough-edged as she thrust the envelope into his hand. 'Take it and read it. It will explain to you exactly what I'm talking about.'

With another of those wary, narrow-eyed looks, Gabriel silently did as he was instructed. Ripping open the letter, he pulled out the sheets of paper it contained and scanned them swiftly. Rachel felt her heart twist in sympathy for Lily, who had agonised so long over choosing what to write, taking such care to select exactly the right words, only to have it read in such a short space of time.

She knew exactly the moment that Gabriel came to

the vital part of his mother's story. His reaction told her just how much it affected him, that it hit him with as much force as it had her when she had first heard it from Lily's own lips.

His dark head went back sharply, moving as if in involuntary rejection of what he had read, then the deep brown eyes moved over the relevant passage once more.

Still with his intent gaze fixed on the letter, he moved unseeingly to the nearest chair and sank down onto it, obviously reading yet again the page he had just finished. Watching him, Rachel found that she was holding her breath almost fearfully, her hands clenched into tight fists, nails digging into her palms as he reached the last paragraph again.

Suddenly Gabriel looked up, brown eyes probing her face.

'What does this mean?' he demanded roughly.

'Exactly what it says.'

Her reply was husky, her voice as croaking and scratchy as if it had seized up with the rest of her body, still held tight in the grip of unbearable tension. Her heart was beating so fast, so high up in her throat that natural breathing was an impossibility.

'But...'

Ebony eyes dazed and clouded, he shook his head in total incredulity.

'Rachel, this letter says that my mother knows you're...'

'That I'm her husband's daughter.' Rachel nodded excited agreement. 'I told her that. But it also says that *you* are not your father's son.'

Her legs, already shaking, now threatened to give way completely, and she sank down onto the arm of the chair beside him, reaching for the letter and pointing out the important passages.

Lily had confessed that in the early days of her marriage she had known of Greg's infidelities and had been so hurt by them that she had almost decided that, if she couldn't beat him, she would join him at his own game. But then she had met a very different sort of man.

An Italian, in England only briefly, he had been much older than her. He had treated her with a gentleness and courtesy that had made her fall madly in love with him in a very short space of time. Her feelings had been returned and they had talked of marriage, of her leaving Greg and going to live in Italy.

But even as she had nerved herself to tell her husband fate had intervened in the form of a sudden, fatal heart attack that had killed her lover instantly. The following week Lily had discovered that she was pregnant with Gabriel. Rachel looked again at the letter.

> I've always known you were Angelo's son. That's why I named you Gabriel, the nearest I dared come to ever actually admitting it. But to be absolutely sure I had blood tests done when you were younger. They proved you could never have been Greg Tiernan's child…

But by then Lily and Greg had been reconciled. Believing the baby she was carrying to be his, he had vowed that he would change, things would be so very different. Knowing that she could never have the happiness she had dreamed of with Angelo, Gabriel's mother had stayed in her marriage, keeping her secret to herself, never telling anyone, not even Gabriel himself—until now.

'So when my father—when Greg had those tests done…' Gabriel was still struggling to take it all in.

'They proved that he was *my* father, but neither of you thought to question if *you* were his son.'

'I wonder…'

His eyes were fixed on a point beyond the window

and he frowned deeply as he tried to recall something important.

'In a letter he wrote to me in America—the letter in which he said he'd decided to make everything all right, and give you a fair share of his estate—he said something then.'

Long fingers massaged his temples, as if to ease an unbearable ache as he concentrated on remembering the details accurately.

'"Rachel's mine, Gabriel," he wrote, "so I'll make sure she gets what's hers by right. That's all that matters. We don't want people probing too deeply into things that don't concern them."'

'So it could be that that's why he didn't tell me. If he had suspected that you might not be his true son, but he'd brought you up all those years as if you were, then he wouldn't have wanted anyone opening that particular can of worms.'

'It looks that way,' Gabriel acknowledged. 'And my mother says here that she kept the truth hidden, even from me, because Greg was the only father I'd ever known. I was registered as his, I'd grown up with him, and there was nothing to be gained by shattering that particular delusion.'

Gabriel rubbed the back of his hand across his forehead, as if by doing so he could force the truth into his still numbed brain.

'And no one ever thought that you and I would need to know about this because we kept our affair so much to ourselves. My mother knew how I felt about you but she always believed you were John Amis's daughter.'

'And now...' Rachel prompted breathlessly, unable to control her excitement any longer. 'Gabriel, you must know what this means for us...'

This wasn't how it was meant to be, she told herself, prey to a dreadful wave of confusion and uncertainty. This wasn't how she'd imagined things when, sitting alone with that vital letter in her hand, she had pictured this moment in her mind.

Then she had dreamed of Gabriel's stunned delight, the overwhelming joy with which he would react to the news that she was not his sister. They were not related in any way, but were free to love each other after all.

She had thought his eyes would sparkle like her own, that his mouth would curve into a wide, brilliant grin, that he would pull her into his arms and kiss her stupid.

But Gabriel had done none of that. Instead, he had remained as distant from her as the moment when he had walked into the room. If anything, he seemed further away than ever. He was reacting as if he had been hit over the head with a steel bar rather than having just been given the best possible news.

'Gabriel!'

Unable to bear it any longer, she bent to press a swift kiss—the prelude to many more, far more satisfying ones, she hoped—against the lean plane of his cheek. His reaction shocked her rigid.

Twisting away from her as if her lips had burned him, he levered himself up out of his seat in a violent movement, his hand coming up defensively before him.

'No!' It was a raw, visceral cry. '*No*, Rachel. I can't!'

'But, Gabriel…'

Rachel got to her feet in a rush, her hand coming out automatically, trying ineffectually to bridge the chasm that seemed to have opened up between them.

'I don't understand. We can be together now. You and I…'

'I *can't*!'

Brushing off her fingers when she would have held him back, he almost ran from the room, leaving her staring after him in shock.

What had happened? Had she got it all wrong after all? Had she been deluding herself when she had thought she had heard that wonderful, passionate declaration of love just days before?

Her heart cried out to go after him, but her head warned against unthinking, impetuous action. Wouldn't that be risking everything? Destroying the small degree of acceptance she had come to after so much pain? Wouldn't it be better, safer, to let sleeping dogs lie?

But then a page from Lily's letter, dropped by Gabriel in his hasty departure, caught her eye. Bending down, she picked it up, reading automatically, swiftly at first, then more slowly, absorbing the importance of what his mother had said.

> Gabriel, my dear, this will all come as a shock to you. You thought you were one person, now you find you're someone else entirely. Everything you believed will be brought into question. You'll have to find yourself again—your father—even me. You'll need time to adjust. Please, I beg of you, take that time and don't do anything rash.

Of course. Rachel's eyes blurred, tears misting over them. In her excitement, her need to have Gabriel know the truth, she had rushed things. She had forgotten the shock it had been to her when Lily had first told her the truth. She had had to have it repeated three times before it had even begun to sink in.

And it was only last night that she had plucked up the courage to tackle her own mother about the way that she, like Lily, had kept the truth of her parentage from her. Lydia had wept a little, and admitted that she would have done anything at all in order to keep Greg's love.

She had promised him not to reveal his secret and had stuck strictly to that promise, even after his death. Greg Tiernan's legacy of tangled relationships still had them all in its grasp, it seemed.

So how much more would that truth affect Gabriel? After all, she had barely endured five days of believing him to be her brother. He had suffered that horror for over five *years*.

She should leave him alone, give him time to get his head round things, but she didn't know if she could bear the wait. An idea suddenly struck her, sending her running upstairs, up to the attic apartment.

Half an hour later she surveyed herself in the mirror with a mixture of satisfaction and embarrassed disbelief. She hadn't realised how much she had changed in five and a half years. She could only hope that Gabriel would think the same. If she dared to go through with this.

A second look in the mirror brought all her doubts rushing back, making her swallow hard. What if she had this all wrong and Gabriel didn't just need time? What if he really didn't want *her*? Wasn't it possible that her attraction had just been that of forbidden fruit, right from the start?

There was only one way to find out. With a million butterflies beating a frantic tattoo inside her stomach, she opened the bedroom door and almost screamed in fright at the sight of the tall, dark, masculine figure who stood on the small landing.

'Steady!'

Gabriel's hand had been lifted to knock at the door, but he swiftly converted the movement into one of support, hard fingers closing over her arm to keep her upright as she swayed on her feet.

'I'm sorry. I didn't think.' He sounded almost as nervous as she felt. 'I was sure you'd have heard me come upstairs.'

'I—my mind was on other things.'

Rachel's breathlessness had nothing to do with the way she had almost fallen but everything to do with his physical closeness, the electric charge his presence seemed to give the air.

'Me too.' It was accompanied by an appealingly attractive lopsided smile. 'I've done a lot of thinking and...Rachel, I'm sorry! I wasn't thinking straight.'

'I understand...'

'I wasn't *thinking* at all, just reacting. I couldn't believe what had happened, couldn't take any of it in. It was all just too much.'

'I know...' Rachel tried again, but, from having held his feelings away from her, he was now so determined to open up that he barely even noticed that she had spoken.

'This must be what it feels like for someone who's been taken hostage and held prisoner for years. They've longed for their freedom, dreamed of it, prayed for it, but when it finally comes they don't know if they can handle it, or even whether to trust it. I was *scared*, Rachel. It seemed too good to be true.'

'Gabriel, I *know*!'

She reached up to clasp his hand, and this time he let his fingers lie easily in her grasp.

'Believe me, I felt something of the same.'

His mouth twisted wryly. 'Yeah, I suppose you must have—'

He stopped suddenly, focusing on her fully for the first time, his expression stunned.

'Rachel, what the *hell* are you wearing?'

'Don't you remember it?'

A new lightness in her heart, Rachel twirled round to show off the silver lace dress she had worn to her nineteenth birthday party.

'Remember it?' His voice was very different, suddenly thick and heavy with new feeling, rich with sensual meaning. 'I've never been able to forget it. But it doesn't look quite as I remember...'

Rachel's laugh was soft and warm as the frankly sensual look in his eyes eased the anxiety of moments before.

'It won't. I've grown up quite a bit since I last wore it.'

'You've certainly done that.'

Ebony eyes lingered at the point where her breasts strained against the tight-fitting lace, sliding downwards to the stretch of the fine material over her hips. If the dress had seemed short five and a half years before, it was now positively indecent.

Which was the effect she had aimed for. But all the same she held her breath, waiting for Gabriel's reaction. This was it. All or nothing. Kill or cure.

'You've grown up and out,' he breathed huskily. 'In all the right places. You don't look the same girl...'

'That's because I'm not her, Gabriel.' Her voice shook with the importance of what she was saying. 'We've both changed a lot since I was nineteen, and, just like this dress, much of our old selves no longer fits properly. We have to get rid of old ways, change how we look at things. We can't go back, only forward—if you want to...'

She couldn't go on. Her eyes pleaded with him to understand, her heart seeming to stand still when he didn't speak, his frown seeming disturbingly ominous. But then it jolted back into frantic action as he nodded his dark head slowly.

'I *want* to,' he said, and there was such a raw need, such a heartfelt passion in the words that it brought swift tears to her eyes. 'Dear God, Rachel, I want it more than anything in the world. I want *you*...'

A deep sigh escaped him as he reached out a hand that was not entirely steady to touch her cheek very gently.

'It's been one hell of a five and a half years, sweetheart. The worst years of my life. All that time, at least as far as I was concerned, you've been wearing a bloody great sign saying "Hands off! Do not touch! Forbidden! Trespassers will very definitely be prosecuted!" I forced myself to hold back, never to think of you in that way ever again. I couldn't just switch from one frame of mind to another, especially when they were so diametrically opposed.'

'I know,' Rachel responded gently. 'I should have thought. I rushed things…'

Her impetuous outburst was hushed by gentle fingers pressed over her lips.

'It's over now,' he said, and the deep intensity of his tone, the burnished flame in the darkness of his eyes, told her that he didn't just mean his shocked response earlier. 'Over for good. And to prove it…'

His mouth replaced his fingers, gentle at first but progressing through warmth to demand, to outright hunger in the space of a couple of heartbeats. Rachel kissed him back, her head swimming with happiness, losing herself in the pure delight until an unexpected clanking noise jolted her back to reality.

'What's that?'

Gabriel's grin was boyish, his eyes glowing with a joy that matched her own, as he lifted his left hand to display the two bottles of champagne that he held by their necks.

'I thought we'd have our own private celebration,' he said, quoting her own words of five and a half years before.

And, hearing them, Rachel felt all the time in between, with its misunderstandings and deceits, its pain and heartbreak, finally melt away, evaporating like the darkest fog before the sun.

'Can we, Rachel? Can we start again? Build a whole new relationship? A new life together?'

For an answer she took hold of his free hand, leading him firmly and confidently into her bedroom. Once inside, she turned and faced him, gently removing the bottles from his grasp and placing them on her dressing table.

'Would I be wrong in assuming that your presence here tonight isn't just a casual visit,' she asked, following his example and quoting his words from that fateful night, when she had come here to what had then been his room, but reversing them, 'but part of a deliberate campaign to make me aware of just how much of a man you are?'

Her smile grew, deepened as she saw his head go back sharply in recognition of what she was doing. It would have been fun to stretch it out, take it step by step exactly as he had done five and a half years before, but she could see his impatience in his eyes and her own hunger was growing every bit as fast. So she decided to skip a line or two.

'Is that it, Gabriel? Do you want me to respond to you as a woman does to a man?'

When Gabriel made an inarticulate sound deep in his throat, she knew once and for all that every one of his doubts had vanished, never to return. Glorying in the way his black gaze was fixed on her, she gave a provocative wriggle, her smile becoming even more brilliant as she saw him swallow hard.

'This dress is way too tight,' she purred, smoothing her hands over its clinging lines, her pulse leaping in anticipation of Gabriel's touch replacing her own, his mouth moving over her body. 'You'll have to help me out of it.'

To her astonishment he shook his head, folding his arms across his chest in adamant refusal to move.

'Wrong line,' he said firmly.

'Wrong…?'

And then it dawned on her. Hastily she thought back, recalling how he had got her to go to him that night.

'Then why don't we dispense with the pussyfooting around?'

Her need put an urgent shake into her voice, her hunger was one that she could see mirrored in the intent darkness of his gaze.

'Drop the pretence that we don't know exactly why you're here...'

She couldn't carry it on any longer. Past caring if she had the right words or not, she abandoned all restraint.

'For God's sake, Gabriel, come here and kiss me!'

His response was lightning-swift. She barely saw him move before he was at her side, kicking the door shut behind him.

'I thought you'd never ask,' he muttered thickly, gathering her up into an embrace that had nothing brotherly about it and everything of the deeply passionate lover. 'We have over five long, empty years to make up for, and I have no intention of wasting another single second.'

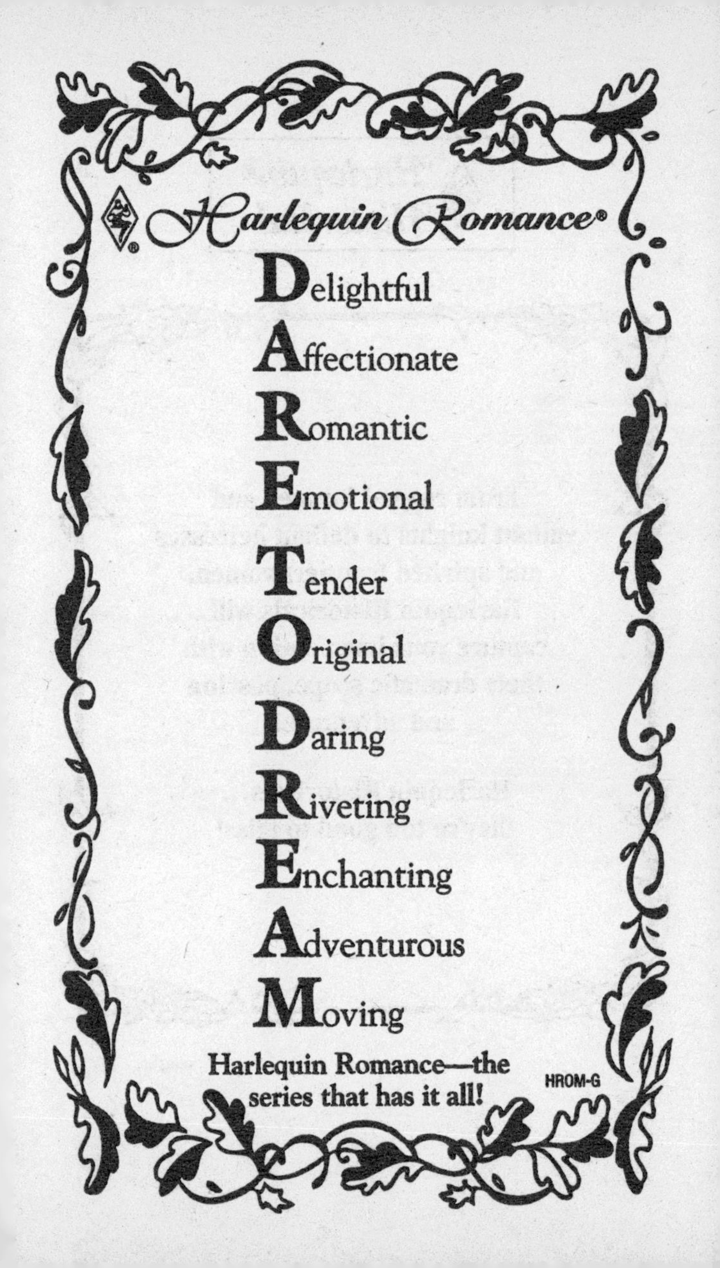
Harlequin Romance®
Delightful
Affectionate
Romantic
Emotional
Tender
Original
Daring
Riveting
Enchanting
Adventurous
Moving
Harlequin Romance—the
series that has it all!
HROM-G